A Pocketful of Stars

A Pocketful of Stars

AISHA BUSHBY

EGMONT

First published in Great Britain 2019
by Egmont UK Limited
The Yellow Building, 1 Nicholas Road, London W11 4AN

Text copyright © 2019 Aisha Bushby

The moral rights of the author and illustrator have been asserted

978 1 4052 9319 8

69013/2

A CIP catalogue record for this title is available
from the British Library

Typeset by Avon DataSet Ltd, Bidford on Avon, Warwickshire
Printed and bound in Great Britain by the CPI Group

For Alfie,

Thank you for braving the world with me - both real and imaginary.

Chapter 1

Mum always turns everything into a game. Even boring days out to the theatre.

'When the play starts,' Mum says, 'count the number of times the cast say Rapunzel's name. Apparently they say it seven times in the first seven minutes!' She pauses, looking between me and my best friend Elle. We glance at each other and frown. 'Seven!' Mum repeats, like this should mean something to us. 'The witching number?' She looks disappointed. 'Oh, never mind.'

I can't help but laugh. Mum's games don't always make sense, because her brain works in mysterious ways.

We're at a coffee shop next door to the theatre, having cake and hot chocolate while we wait to watch an afternoon performance of *Rapunzel*.

'Fine, you think of a better game to play while we watch,'

she says, chucking her napkin at me, grinning.

'We could just watch the play?' I offer.

Mum snorts, shaking her head. 'Boring.'

'OK, fine.' I think for a moment. 'How about we count the number of times the cast says "hair"?' I suggest. 'Isn't that what the story is about?'

It's Mum's turn to laugh. '*Rapunzel* isn't about hair!' she says. 'I've never heard something so ridiculous. It's about freedom, and independence, and exploring the world.'

While Mum talks, I look up a line from the story on my phone and read it out, smirking. '"Rapunzel, Rapunzel, let down thy hair." You have to admit, Mum, it does seem to be about hair . . .'

'Cheeky,' Mum says, taking a sip of her coffee. 'Anyway, what about you, Elle, what do you think we should count?'

Elle, who's been watching us talk back and forth like a referee at a tennis match, chimes in. 'We've been doing Shakespeare at school this year, and apparently whenever anyone performs *Macbeth*, it's bad luck to say his name in the theatre before the play!'

Mum looks genuinely interested. 'Yes, I have heard this! But also, did you know . . .' And soon enough Mum and Elle have launched into a conversation about different traditions in the theatre – something I could never talk about.

Elle's like a chameleon, she always knows what to say. She changes personalities depending on who she's around and can talk to just about anyone, like Mum. I'm just a plain old lizard, darting into the corner of every room I enter.

While they talk, I get distracted by the countdown on my phone. *Fifteen minutes.*

That's when tickets to the biggest video gaming convention of the year are released. Dad promised he would go with me if I could get us both tickets. I've been saving up my birthday money for it.

The thing is, they can sometimes sell out in minutes, so you have to be quick.

'Hurry up, Safiya!' Mum calls. I look up and find her at the door of the coffee shop tapping her feet, impatient to leave.

Mum and I look so similar we could almost be twins, apart from our hair and my glasses. We both have olive skin and brown eyes. Except Mum has black curls that float down her back, whereas my hair hangs by my waist in limp waves.

'Mum, the play doesn't start for another half-hour,' I protest. Secretly I want to stay here long enough to buy the tickets before we go inside. But if I tell Mum that she won't understand.

'I want to find our seats early, get comfortable!'

'And that takes half an hour?'

Mum sighs, opens her mouth to retort, and then storms out of the coffee shop.

I can't help but roll my eyes. Mum can be so hot and cold sometimes, like a sunny winter's day. Things can be going really well, then suddenly everything changes.

The truth is, even though Mum and I look alike, we're not very similar in other ways. Often it's like we're on different pages of the same book, always just missing each other as the page turns.

'Come on, Saff,' Elle says, reaching for my hand. She's used to mine and Mum's bickering now.

When we get into the theatre foyer it's packed, and I walk with Elle until we find Mum outside the hall, tickets in hand. She hasn't seen us yet.

Elle says she's going to pop to the toilets quickly so I stop, for a moment, and watch Mum standing there alone. Her eyes are far away, like they're in a different world entirely. Mum's been so intense about this show, more than I've ever seen her before. You'd think we were going to the West End, not the local theatre in our tiny town.

A member of staff approaches her and Mum's eyes focus again. 'No thank you,' she says when the woman asks if she needs any help. 'I'm just waiting for my daughter and her friend.' Then she comments on how lovely the woman's earrings are and her face lights up as she tells Mum that she made them herself. Soon enough they're in a full-blown conversation about jewellery-making, even though Mum knows nothing about it.

Mum's good at talking to people, being a lawyer. She

4

knows exactly what to say at all times. I'm different. I only know how to express myself in video games. Instead of words, I use spells and incantations.

Once the woman leaves, Mum's face falls into a frown. She checks her watch and glances anxiously across the foyer, just as Elle taps me on the shoulder. Then Mum sees us. Except she sees Elle before me, because she stands out way more than I do, with her bright red mane like a beacon of light.

'There you are!' Mum says, relieved, but I can hear the annoyance in her voice too.

I check the time. Five minutes until the convention tickets are released.

'I'm just going to the toilet!' I say. 'Be back in a second.'

Mum lets out a noise that sounds like a monster is living inside her. She hands me my ticket, barely looking at me now. 'You'll have to find your seat alone,' she warns, like I'm five years old, and not thirteen.

Once Mum and Elle have disappeared inside the hall I run back outside the theatre and into the coffee shop again, where they have Wi-Fi. I log in to my account and watch the countdown.

Two minutes.

'Did you want a drink?' the person behind the counter asks.

I stare at him blankly.

'You're not really supposed to be in here without a

drink,' he clarifies, a little more sternly.

I hate being told off.

My eyes dart between the coffee-shop guy and the countdown on my phone, and I panic, frozen. I try to open my mouth but it's like it's glued shut. I am not good under pressure with strangers. So I just shake my head and run back out on to the street.

Stupid, Saff, I think, feeling embarrassed. If Mum or Elle were here they would have been able to talk to him and say, 'Yes, just an orange juice please,' and buy the tickets to the gaming convention, and everything would be fine.

Instead I stand on the street for fifteen minutes, where the Wi-Fi doesn't work, and there's hardly any signal. I try to load the page over and over, until all the tickets have sold out and the page shows a big sad smiley face with a pop-up bubble that says 'Maybe next year'.

To make everything worse, by the time I get back to the theatre the play's already started. Mum's going to be furious!

I slip into my seat after stepping on about five people's toes, almost knocking a drink out of someone's hand, and getting a few tuts from older men and women. And when I'm finally in my seat I shrink so low I'm surprised I haven't morphed into a turtle, hiding inside its shell.

I look over at Elle and she gives me a small thumbs up, before turning back to the play. Mum's next to her on the other side, ignoring me. I watch the two of them whisper to each other during the play like best friends.

At the interval Mum goes and grabs her and Elle an ice cream – vanilla for Mum, strawberry for Elle. She doesn't ask me, even though she knows chocolate is my favourite.

'Sorry,' she says. 'I didn't realize you wanted one. We both said we would get them before the play started, but you weren't here.'

Mum's all smiles and warmth, but her eyes are a warning, like a lioness ready to pounce.

'Anyway, did you count?' Mum asks, turning to Elle.

'Yes!' Elle says. 'You were right.'

Mum nods, satisfied.

When the play is over I'm the first out. I wait for Mum and Elle, but they take ages.

'Saff, your mum said I could come round tonight for dinner,' Elle says when she finally catches up with me.

'We're going to watch *The Wizard of Oz*,' Mum chimes in. 'It's my favourite, Elle. You'll like it, I think. I'd love to see the theatre performance of *Wicked* one day . . .'

Elle and Mum walk off, talking about the rest of the play, heads bobbing enthusiastically. I hang back a step or two. They're both confident, so it makes sense that they get along, that their relationship is easy. I should be glad, but it's a bit like playing my favourite video game, *Fairy Hunters*, and my team wins even though I didn't cast a single good spell. I want to be happy, but then I feel like I don't belong, like I'm not good enough. And the bad feeling takes over the good.

I know it's weird not wanting Elle to come round, because she's my best friend. But Saturday nights are supposed to be our night. Mum and me.

Ever since Mum and Dad divorced, and I decided to live with Dad, they set up these Saturday visits as part of the custody agreement. Mum and I hang out in the afternoon, and then we have dinner together and a sleepover. Usually Mum cooks, sometimes it's a takeaway, but it's always just been the two of us.

Until today.

I can't help but think that maybe Elle's the daughter Mum should've had, the daughter she would've wanted.

But instead she ended up with me.

Chapter 2

'**R**oar!' I growl, leaping out from behind a mirror.

Elle squeals and giggles and then she hides behind a rail of clothes.

We're shopping in London today, using vouchers from our Christmas presents. I found a big fur coat so, naturally, I put it on and pretended to be a bear.

Abir and Izzy widen their eyes at one another, as if to say 'how immature', but I catch Izzy grinning at me.

'You're so funny, Saff,' Abir says a little flatly, in a way that suggests the exact opposite.

I ignore her. She takes herself a bit too seriously sometimes.

'Hey, Saff!' Elle calls from across the shop. A couple of older shoppers look on disapprovingly as Elle gallops across in a zebra jacket, and suddenly I feel like shy Saff again, worried they'll tell us off the way that man did at the coffee shop last week.

The truth is, I've been trying to distract myself from everything going on today. This is the first Saturday in ages that I haven't seen Mum. Last week, after we got back from the theatre and Elle had gone home, we had an argument – a *horrid* argument – and I stormed out of Mum's flat. She never called or texted afterwards, and I didn't text her either, so I assumed I wasn't going round today.

I glance at my phone. Nothing. And somehow that hurts more than Mum's angry words. Suddenly I feel annoyed all over again. I switch off my phone, as if to get back at her for ignoring me.

'OK, let's be serious now,' Abir says, like we're running some sort of covert operation. 'Meet at the changing rooms in half an hour, yeah?'

'Come on, Saff,' Elle says, grabbing my hand and leading the way. 'I need your help.'

I follow Elle obediently, just as I followed her on the second day of primary school. She decided we were going to be a snake, right in the middle of the playground. Elle, of course, was the snake's head. I was behind her, hands on her shoulders. I felt silly and embarrassed at the time. Everyone was going to laugh at us, I was sure. But Elle was confident. She hissed and ran and giggled, and soon half of the playground joined us. Elle at the front, me following right behind. And that's how it's been ever since.

When we're alone again we fall into that easy sort of conversation we have when it's just the two of us. Sometimes we even forget where we are because the Saff and Elle bubble is indestructible – even an army of goblins couldn't break through it.

I ask Elle what she's been reading, and she asks me about gaming. I tell her that I just ranked up on *Fairy Hunters*, and she describes a series of books about an undercover alchemist. It's set in a boarding school, like *Harry Potter*, and sounds really cool. We agree to have a three-day sleepover, where we binge on our favourite TV shows and films over half-term, and never change out of our pyjamas.

Later, when we stop for some food, Elle gets a message. 'It's your dad,' she says, frowning, showing me her screen. 'He wants you to look at your phone.'

That's weird. Why would Dad message Elle? As soon as I see the stream of missed calls, voice messages and texts I know something's wrong.

Dad: [Missed Call]
Dad: Saff, can you call me as soon as you get this?
Dad: [Missed Call]
Dad: [Missed Call]
Dad: Can you catch the next train home?

I know something big has happened, and I know when I find out that everything will be different.

I grab Elle's hand and squeeze, like maybe it'll stop time. She squeezes back. I wordlessly hand her my phone and wait for her to tell me what to do.

'We'll go now, OK?' she says, before turning to the others to explain. 'See you later, yeah?'

Abir and Izzy nod solemnly. I hear them whisper to Elle and ask her what's going on, but I don't hear her response. I don't even say goodbye.

We leave in a rush, our food half eaten, and head to Tube station.

I quickly text Dad before we go on the Underground. My hands are shaking.

'Shall we ring your dad first?' Elle asks.

I shake my head. I can't here. Not now. I need everything to stop, just for a little while. Because the truth is, I don't want to know what Dad has to say.

Saff: Getting on the Tube. I'll ring you from the train. Be about 20 mins.

Elle holds my hand the whole way down, even as we go through the barriers.

Four stops to King's Cross. Four stops for me to imagine the worst. Dad must be OK. I don't have any grandparents, or aunts and uncles, apart from Mum's sister . . . Is it Mum?

One. Mum cycles everywhere. Did she get hit by a car? Does she wear a helmet? I can't remember.

Elle and I don't speak. She just squeezes my arm every few moments. I don't cry, but my heart is beating so fast I feel like I can't breathe.

The Tube is too hot. I might pass out.

Two. Maybe she just tripped and broke a leg, and I'm overthinking it all? Dad's just ringing to make sure I don't go straight to her flat. Right?

But why is he telling me to get the next train?

Someone gets up and Elle wrestles me a seat.

Three. And why would he ring Elle too?

I bury my head in my hands. Elle is stroking my hair. It helps.

Four. I'm sorry for yelling at you, Mum. I'm sorry, sorry, sorry.

'When's our train?' I ask as we step off the Tube.

'Ten minutes. We'll make it.'

But I'm not so sure we will. I feel like a broken puppet, my strings hanging uselessly by my side, with no control over my legs or arms. As we make our way up the escalators I walk around in a daze. Eventually Elle picks up my strings and leads me, like all those years ago.

I don't recall going through the ticket barrier, searching for our platform, or making my way on to the train.

But suddenly I'm in my seat and my phone is in my hand. Dad's contact details are up on my screen.

'You can do this,' Elle says, squeezing my hand. And it's like time has started all over again.

I call Dad.

The phone rings.

And rings.

He doesn't answer.

The train is filled with excitable children, fuelled by sweets and fizzy drinks. They laugh and it sounds weird. Wrong. I want to switch places with them, to pretend everything's OK. How are they so happy, so full of life when mine feels like it's about to end? I watch two of them chase each other, giggling uncontrollably. But then one of them accidentally trips the other and suddenly both of them are in tears, each of their parents cuddling them for comfort.

Elle and I find a quiet corner and watch the world go by as the train pulls away from the station.

My phone vibrates in my hand moments into the journey. My fingers ache from squeezing it so tightly. 'Hello?' I say, my voice shaky.

'Safiya?'

'Dad, what's happened?' I ask. There are already tears in my eyes ready to fall. I take a deep breath, and then another.

'It's your mum,' he says, and it's like a lead brick slams hard against my abdomen. 'She's . . .'

Dead, I think. *Just say it. Just tell me.* But I can't speak.

' . . . in a coma.'

'But she's alive?' I wipe my eyes and cheeks with the sleeve of my coat.

14

I can sense Elle's body stiffen, as she connects the dots of the one-sided conversation she's hearing.

'Yes.' Dad exhales as he speaks. 'Where are you now?'

'On the train. I'll be at the station soon.'

'OK. I'll pick you up. I tried to see her but it's too soon for visitors.'

'Dad?'

'Yes, Saff?'

'H-how . . . What happened?'

'They think it was a stroke,' Dad admits, his voice shaky. 'I don't know anything more just yet.'

I nod, and then realize he can't see me. 'OK,' I say. It comes out strangled, more a wail than a word. More tears follow. They fall easily now.

The ticket lady starts to make her way down the carriage. 'Tickets, passes and railcards!'

'I have to go now,' Dad says. 'I'll speak to the doctor, then head straight to the train station. Are you with Elle?'

I swallow before replying; it's like gulping down a stone.

'Tickets, passes and railcards!'

'Saff?'

'Yes, I'm with her.' I wipe snot on my sleeve.

'Good. Not long now, I promise.'

I put the phone down and stare ahead at the chair in front of me. A piece of mint-green chewing gum is lodged between the back of the seat and the tray.

'Tickets, passes and railcards!' the woman repeats,

15

marching down the aisle with purpose. When she reaches us Elle whispers something to her.

She glances at me before nodding at Elle.

'Come on,' Elle says, grabbing my arm and my things. We crawl to the back of the train, my vision blurred from the tears. She slides a door open, and it's only when I walk through and feel the heat that I realize she's lead me to the posh carriage.

No one's in here, just us.

'Is your mum . . . ?' she asks, trailing off. 'Is she . . . ?'

'She's in a coma.' I whisper the words, testing them out on my tongue.

And that's when I know things will never be the same again.

Chapter 3

The next day we're at the hospital I was born in. We couldn't see Mum last night because the doctors were busy operating on her brain. For some reason, when I imagine it happening, all I can think of is that old-school game, Operation, where you have to remove different body parts without setting off the buzzer.

They called Dad this morning to let him know how it went, and to say that we would be able to visit Mum in the afternoon. So, I guess, the buzzer never went off. It's not GAME OVER.

'She's in the intensive care unit,' Dad explains, leading the way.

We follow the yellow line on the wall like Dorothy and the Scarecrow on their way to Oz. Except, instead of the Wizard, we're going to see Mum.

My mouth is all dry and I feel sick. It doesn't help that

everything smells like antiseptic.

Still, we walk and walk and walk, until we turn a corner where a reception desk sits in the semi-darkness, surrounded by rooms.

'James and Safiya Fisher to see Aminah Al-Adwani,' Dad says.

Aminah. I forget that's her name sometimes. I'm so used to her being Mum.

'Are you a relation?' the nurse asks. I look down at his badge and read the name Edward Hussein.

'I'm her ex-husband, but I'm still her emergency contact. I was, uh, I was here yesterday.'

Edward nods at Dad before turning to me, a sad smile on his face. 'And you must be her daughter?'

I swallow, and it's like a great big stone is sliding down my throat landing, *thud*, in my chest. I can feel it right next to my heart.

'If you could both take a seat, I'll call you when she's ready,' he says, like Mum's just in a meeting.

I don't want to speak, so I play on my phone to distract myself.

Elle messages me just as I'm feeding my pets on this new app I downloaded. Lady, our Cavalier King Charles spaniel, would be horrified if she knew about my virtual cat. She gets jealous pretty easily. Once I had to look after our class hamster for the weekend, and I swear Lady wouldn't look me in the eye for days after.

Elle: Hope you're OK xxxxxx

Safiya: Going to see her in a minute. I'm scared. Xxxx

Elle's message makes it all real again, and suddenly I can't play the game any more.

In the next room there's an old man lying in one of the hospital beds alone. He stares at the same spot on the ceiling for ages, and all I can think about is how no one is there to see him. And then I think about how I wasn't there to see Mum yesterday at her flat, before she was called into hospital – all because of our argument.

'That's so silly, Safiya,' Mum had said when I explained that I didn't want to join the local theatre group. 'Gaming isn't a hobby . . . Hobbies require you to leave the comfort of your own room.' She laughed, even though it wasn't funny. 'I would understand all this if you were a bit younger, but you're in Year Eight now.'

'James? Safiya?' Edward calls for us. I jump, but I don't stand. I can't. For a moment my body doesn't respond to my brain.

I turn to Dad, who is about to stand up.

I put my hand on his shoulder. 'Is it OK if I go alone?'

I've been so used to it just being Mum and me, without Dad, that it would be weird to be the three of us again.

Dad frowns at me for a moment, and I think he's going to say no, but then his face softens and he squeezes me

19

back. I turn round, take a deep breath, and follow Edward.

He leads me to the entrance and uses a special key card to open the doors. Then he gives me some quick instructions: *walk straight to the end and turn right.*

It makes me think of *Peter Pan* and how they all get to Neverland. *'Second star to the right, and straight on till morning.'*

Except, instead of going to Neverland, I'm going to see Mum.

'Would you like me to come with you?' Edward asks.

I shake my head. Adults can't go to Neverland.

I walk through and it's like everything is happening in slow motion.

Doctors and nurses walk past me, barely glancing in my direction. I turn back and see Dad's face as the doors close behind me. He gives me a small smile, which makes me feel a little bit stronger.

I rolled my eyes. 'I knew you would say this,' I countered. 'Because you just don't get it, do you?'

Mum crossed her arms. 'Grow up, Safiya,' she said. 'You aren't some mystery to me, you know. I know what it's like to be your age. When I was younger I –'

I didn't let her finish her sentence. Instead it was my turn to laugh. 'Were you ever my age?' I said. 'Sometimes I just imagine you were always old with your boring job and your boring life.'

That stopped Mum in her tracks. Then she started again, and suddenly she was a moving train, picking up momentum.

'*You have no idea what I've had to do to get this job. I left home when I wasn't much older than you, studied hard . . .*'

What else did she say? I can't remember, because I wasn't listening.

The walk along the hospital corridor takes a million years. I have to remind myself how to move my feet.

Left. Right. Left. Right.

I pause at the halfway point. I can see Mum's room now at the end. Sometimes, when I play an especially scary game, I save it just before something really bad happens, and do something else for a while, until I have the courage to face it. If this were a game I would click save and take Lady for a walk instead. But I can't, so I just lean against the hospital wall. It's cracked, the paint chipped and worn. It feels as if the whole building might tumble down, down, down and take me with it.

Mum sank down on to the sofa, her head in her hands. I thought for a moment that she was crying.

'*I've got a splitting headache . . .*' *she said, rubbing her temples.*

I thought it was an excuse, a way to stop us fighting.

So instead of backing down, I kept pushing; maybe this time I could win. And I picked the button I knew would hurt most.

'*Dad gets it,*' *I said, relishing the way my words made Mum flinch.* '*He was going to take me to a gaming convention this summer. But then you took us to that stupid play, and I missed*

21

out on tickets.'

'Oh, Safiya,' Mum said, sounding annoyed now. She was still massaging her head. 'Why did you come then if you hated it so much? Elle seemed to enjoy herself . . .'

I shrugged. 'Because I had to.'

I could tell that upset Mum, but she swallowed down the hurt and carried on.

'Look, I know you get along better with your father.' I could taste the bitterness in her voice. 'You don't half remind me of it every day. But maybe you could just push yourself a little and –'

'Just stop it, Mum!' I interrupted. 'I'm not going to the theatre group,' I said with finality. 'I don't want to.'

Was it my fault? Did this happen because I upset her?

I want to ask the doctors these questions, but I'm too afraid of the answers.

I'm now right in front of the door to Mum's hospital room. It's open, just a crack. And then I see her face. My heart jolts and I turn away. I sit on an abandoned chair outside, head in my hands, blocking out the rest of the argument.

I shut my eyes, take my glasses off, and press the palms of my hands hard against my eyelids, until white spots form against the black. I try to erase the picture of Mum in her hospital bed, to go back to a point before all this happened. I imagine that I'm staring at the solar system, and I try to believe – really believe – that I'm somewhere far away.

A while later I'm still sitting there, eyes trained on the floor now, avoiding the door. A nurse walks out, letting out a startled 'Oh!' It's almost comical, the way she jumps back. All I see are her white shoes acting out her surprise.

'I'm sorry,' I say, wiping the tears that now fall freely down my face. 'My m-mum is in there and I c-c-c-' I break into sobs, barely able to breathe.

The nurse kneels in front of me, but I don't look her in the eye. Instead I stare at her name badge, which says 'Amanda' on it.

'Deep breaths,' Amanda says. 'Come on, darling, you can do this. Breathe with me.'

She inhales, holding her hand to her chest, and I copy her. She exhales and I follow.

After a few moments I'm breathing normally again. Someone else comes to bring me a cup of water. It tastes metallic and I only sip enough to wet my lips.

I put my glasses back on, stand up and turn back to the door, making sure to keep focused on the wheels of Mum's bed, and not her face.

'Are you sure?' Amanda asks.

I nod.

'OK.' She leads me in and guides me to Mum's bed. 'I'm going to slide the curtains shut, give you some privacy, but I'll be on the other side if you need me. All right?'

'Thank you,' I mumble.

Amanda looks at me for a moment, before shutting the

curtains behind her.

It takes me a full minute to look up at Mum once we're alone.

Slowly I move my eyes up from the base of her bed, across the thin sheets that cover her legs, all the way up to her hands and the tubes attached to the back of them, and finally to her face.

The first thing I think is how great she looks. It sounds odd, but she does. Her skin is almost glowing. Right now, there aren't any dark circles to show the hours of staying up late working at her computer, no frown lines to shape her concentration, and her mouth isn't downturned in disappointment, the way it often is when we speak.

I'm sorry I was so horrible, I think, but I can't say it aloud.

Every time Mum and I argue about one thing, three or four previous arguments get dragged into it. We've now battled out each of our issues so many times that they no longer make sense. We've never managed to resolve anything either, so our problems just grow and grow, like a monster that feeds off our frustration with one another.

It wasn't like this before secondary school. Saturdays used to be fun. We would play and laugh, and Mum liked me for me. But then it changed, and now it's like I can't do anything right.

Our last argument felt like it grew so big that the monster had taken over Mum's flat entirely, suffocating us both.

Mum looks relaxed now, almost like she's smiling. Like

24

she has a secret.

Her long, brown hair is fanned out across the pillow, her curls perfectly placed. She looks like Sleeping Beauty, hands clasped over her chest, waiting for the kiss of life.

Without thinking, I stand up, lean over her, and stroke strands of hair away from her face. The smell of her musky perfume has somehow managed to linger on her skin, even after everything that's happened. It makes my chest tighten.

Mum's had the same perfume since I can remember. It's surrounded every hug she's given me. But we don't hug much any more and I'd forgotten how much I missed it.

I kiss her on her forehead and my tears sink into her skin.

I sit back and wait for the magic to happen.

But this isn't a fairy tale, and princesses don't wake up after kisses.

Chapter 4

'*Wake up,*' something whispers into the darkness. '*Safiya, wake up.*'

When I next open my eyes I'm lying on my back staring up at the sky. The stars wink at me, brighter than I've seen them before. There are thousands of them, millions, coating the land like a great big blanket. The moon greets me shyly in a crescent wave.

I sit up. It takes a while for my eyes to adjust, for me to get my bearings. I'm in some sort of courtyard.

It's hot, hotter than I've ever known it. Like opening the oven door just after you've baked something delicious. I almost expect my glasses to fog. The smells are wild and sweet.

Wood. Rose, maybe? And orange.

I look up to see an enormous house staring back at me. *Where am I?*

Silver branches scale the house walls, covering almost every inch of it. They bleed into the windows and out of the doors.

They sway, like blades of grass in the breeze, and tap at the glass of the windows, as if asking to be let in. Except there is no wind. The night is as dry as lavender sprigs. Looking closer I can see the branches are as thick as a snake, with leaves like gnarled fingers protruding from them.

They reach out for me, and that's when I see they're not swaying at all, but wriggling like little worms.

I swear I can hear them whisper my name. '*Safiya*,' they hiss. '*Safiya, welcome.*'

I shudder, step back, and look around me.

This is the biggest house I've ever seen, about the size of the block of flats Mum lives in.

There's a set of swings to the right of me, a couple of cars parked in front of it, and a great big iron gate to my left leading out on to the road.

How did I get here?

I try to think back to the last thing I was doing. But it's as if the memory is just out of reach. My brain feels foggy, like I've just woken up. Moving around is strange too, like when I step I'm floating, instead of walking. I wave my hand in front of my face and I can see it blur a little.

That's when I remember what I was doing, and the realization comes crashing down like hailstones. I was sitting by Mum's hospital bed. But then how did I get here? And where am I? I need to leave this place. *I'm trespassing after all*, I think, looking at the big iron gate.

Once, when Elle and I were little, we snuck into her neighbour's garden. It wasn't *exactly* our fault.

We were playing Frisbee and it flew into the vegetable patch next door. It started off with us jumping over the fence to go and get it, but then Elle turned to me.

'It's like being in *The Secret Garden*, isn't it?'

She was right. This wasn't like any normal vegetable patch. It was *huge*, taller than both of us. We played hide-and-seek, and pretended we were Jack, climbing up the beanstalk into giant territory. Except a very real giant – or so we imagined at the time – in the form of Elle's neighbour threatened to call the police when he saw us there.

'I was just getting my Frisbee,' Elle said sweetly.

It worked, and we didn't even get in trouble.

Still, Elle's not here right now, even though I wish she was.

She would know what to do.

I rush towards the gate and pull it open with a great big creak. But it's almost as if something is trying to pull me back, like an elastic band stretching as far as it can go.

And I swear I hear a voice whisper, '*Come back, Safiya.*'

But when I turn round to see who spoke, no one's there.

I'm not sure what to do with myself once I'm away from the house. There are rows of equally giant houses to my left and right, a park across the street framed with palm trees, and a corner shop that sits on the other side of it.

It seems to be open. Maybe I can ask them to tell me where I am. Maybe they can explain why it's so hot, why there are trees I've never seen in England before, and why I keep hearing someone call my name.

I don't seem to have anything on me, even though I could swear my phone was in my pocket when I got to the hospital.

I run across the street, eyes darting left and right, looking out for people and cars. But as my foot hits the pavement on the other side of the road, the corner shop starts to shake and crumble. The roof sinks in and the walls tumble down, down, down, like a sandcastle washed away by the ocean.

The park turns to ash. Replacing it is a barren wasteland of sand for miles, mounds of it everywhere.

I turn round, but the house has disappeared too.

Before I have the chance to panic I hear another voice, a different one this time.

'Visiting hours are over, love,' someone says from a distance.

Chapter 5

I whip my head up. I had been sitting next to Mum's hospital bed, my head resting just next to her right arm.

'Sorry to wake you,' the nurse, Amanda, adds. I try to make sense of my surroundings again. 'I'll give you five minutes,' she says, before retreating behind the curtain.

What a strange dream, I think as I try to reorient myself. It felt so real – like a hallucination, or something. Every time I blink it feels like I'm still in it, like my body and mind has been split into two. It was warm there, and I feel hot in my coat, even though it's freezing outside.

From the corner of my eye I see silver branches crawling up the wall and along the floor, reaching for me. I look down and see sand. But then I blink and I see the branches are only wires from Mum's monitor, and the sand is the shine from the fluorescent lighting.

I try to shake off my sense of panic, but it feels as if there are party poppers going off in my chest. I check my phone. It's been twenty minutes since Elle texted me. How did so much happen in that time?

A violent shiver passes through me as I make to leave, and suddenly I can feel the midwinter chill again. It's like I've been dunked in ice-cold water. It slams against my chest and for a second I can't breathe.

I lean against the curtain rail next to Mum's bed. My limbs feel tingly, like they're not quite attached to me, and my head is swirling with the dream.

Eventually, after I say goodbye to Mum, I make my way back to the reception desk, where I find Dad, and notice again the room with the old man in it. It feels like a lifetime since I first saw him. A young woman and two children surround him now. He's chatting and smiling with her while they play with the settings on his bed. He has a pile of books on his bedside and a tartan blanket by his feet. They make the room look alive.

I'll bring some of Mum's things next time, I think.

When we get home I still feel a little strange. I wave my hand in front of my face and I swear it blurs, just like in the dream. It makes me wonder if I'm still asleep. I blink once, then twice, and hope that everything becomes normal again. But nothing's normal any more, is it?

I want so much to go back to last week, before everything

31

went wrong. We're going to see Mum again tomorrow after school, but what am I supposed to do until then?

My feet tread the familiar path up to my room, and I automatically jump on to my computer, without really meaning to. But as soon as my headphones are on, it feels like the rest of the world disappears.

ENTER GAME

I click on the button, which resembles an old scroll, and wait for the screen to load.

My bedroom walls pull apart brick by brick, and in their place sprouts an ancient fairy palace; my bed folds up into a giant nest; and, instead of street lamps and terraced houses, my windows show me a dense forest as tall as the eye can see. And, all at once, I feel calm.

The world of *Fairy Hunters* unfolds around me. I've been playing it since I was ten, and I'm getting pretty good at it now. It's an online game where you're put into teams to battle it out – fairies against wizards. I always choose Team Fairy. The aim of the game is to protect our nest of eggs from the wizards, who try to steal them to make potions.

There are four kinds of fairy on each team – earth, fire, water and wind. Earth fairies are the protectors; they go in first as they have the best defensive spells to protect their team. Then come the fire fairies – the close-range spellcasters. They need to cast quickly and attack the wizards before they have the chance to defend themselves. Next are the water fairies, the long-range spellcasters. Their job is to cast spells that take more time to conjure but are more powerful. They usually hang back. Then there are the wind fairies. I'm one of them. Our job is to help the rest of the team. Most people don't like playing as wind fairies, because they think we're useless.

We're not. A lot of the time we're the difference between winning and losing the game.

As I walk through the map and see the ruined palace in the distance – ivy growing all over it, walls cracked – I can't help but remember the house from my dream with the silver branches. The park, too, looks similar. Except, instead of palm trees, in *Fairy Hunters*, the trees are oak; and, instead of a corner shop, there's the Wicked Woodlands where the wizards live.

Almost an hour later I'm just about to be crowned most valuable player when Dad's voice floats up from the living room beneath me. 'Safiya!' he calls, piercing the bubble that my headphones have formed. 'Dinner!'

And, just like that, the spell is broken.

Chapter 6

The next day at school everything's a little strange. The teachers keep talking to me in really high-pitched voices, eyes creased with sympathy. It's the way strangers talk to Lady in the street. Usually she wees on them in response. She does that a lot when people are nice to her.

As I was getting ready to leave Maths for lunch Ms Belgrave called me over, handed me a pack of sweets and winked, like it was a secret. Except, instead of winking she kind of just twitched her eye. I didn't wee on her, the way Lady would, I just took the sweets and said thank you.

I suppose Dad will have told the teachers about Mum, but that doesn't explain why everyone else is staring at me. I keep checking to see if I have toilet roll on my shoe or a giant spot in the middle of my nose.

'What do you think, Saff?' Elle asks halfway through lunch.

I turn to her, eyes wide. I realize I haven't been listening. I'd been thinking about the strange dream I had at the hospital yesterday.

Izzy saves me. 'I think he's cool,' she says.

That's when I realize they're talking about Matty Chung, Elle's latest crush. I glance over at him, where he sits with his best friends Jonnie and David.

I don't know how to respond because I don't really think anything of him, or any boys, for that matter.

I remember when we were in Year Seven and no one else talked to us. Sounds weird, but I preferred it. We used to have a sleepover at Elle's house every Friday night. We would do our homework first while Elle's mum baked. It was usually cookies or a cake that she would let us have as a treat before dinner. Afterwards we always watched a film and then stayed up late chatting or playing silly games in bed when we were supposed to be sleeping.

But then Year Eight happened, and we made more friends, and now everyone wants to hang out at Maccies after school or go to the cinema with boys. Everything's changing so quickly that it feels like my world is crumbling, just like in the dream. Like everything I've ever known is made of sand; one big wave could wash it away into the ocean.

'Saff!' Elle whispers furiously. 'Don't stare at him. He'll know we're talking about him.'

'Sorry.' I smile sheepishly and turn back to my lasagne.

'What's the latest anyway?' Elle asks. 'How's your mum?'

Three pairs of eyes turn to me just then, and I want to shrink away from their sympathy, hide from their curiosity.

'I don't really know,' I admit, playing with my food. 'Mum's in a coma still. Apparently she had some sort of stroke. There's a fancy name for it, but I can't really remember it now.'

What I *do* know is that being in a coma is kind of like you're asleep, except you can't be woken up by loud noises or dogs licking your face in the morning.

Often the patient – which is how they keep referring to Mum – wakes up after a few weeks, once their body has recovered from the trauma. I don't think about the other outcome, which is that some patients never wake up.

The doctors asked Dad and me if Mum had any symptoms in the weeks leading up to the stroke. The main symptom, they explained, was a headache about a week or two before.

My heart dropped when they said that, because Mum had complained about a headache during our argument. And then I'd . . .

I didn't tell the doctors about it, though, because that would mean I would have to tell them about the argument, and I don't know if I could bear to find out that it was all my fault.

'She had an operation on the first night, so now all we

can do is . . . wait,' I finish lamely.

Waiting feels so . . . wrong. I want to *do* something, to help. But instead I just have to live life like normal.

Dad said it was important to maintain my routine, whatever that means, and carry on with school and friends. But why pretend everything's fine when it's all wrong, wrong, wrong?

Suddenly tears well up in my eyes.

'D-does anyone want some sweets?' I ask to avoid the embarrassment of crying. 'Ms Belgrave gave them to me,' I add, accidentally spilling the contents all over the table.

'Oh, Saff!' Elle says, grabbing my hand. Izzy goes to get a tissue, while Abir strokes my shoulder. 'We're here for you. Anything you need . . .'

I nod. 'Thank you.' I smile back at them, even though I want to keep crying.

I try to focus on *doing* something, instead of sitting here and moping. That's when I get an idea.

'Actually . . .' I say. 'There is something you could do for me . . .'

A little while later I leave school just before the bell rings for the end of lunch. I asked Elle and the others to let our form tutor know I've gone home.

Except that's not really where I'm going.

With shaking hands I put the key in the lock and let myself inside. My first thought is that it's really quiet. Usually the

TV is on, or some music. I switch on the lights, take off my coat, and turn on the TV for background noise. My second thought is that it smells like her – Mum's flat.

It's a full minute, maybe more, before I can bear to step inside any further. It's as if I'm glued to the door, paralysed, like a wizard has trapped me in a snare. My blood is pumping around my body too quickly and I feel my limbs tingling, too heavy to lift. I crouch down at the threshold for a moment until the feeling passes.

The living room's a bit of a mess. The house phone is on the floor. Dad said Mum called the ambulance herself. She could tell something was happening to her. The coffee table has been shoved aside – that must have been the paramedics. Then there's papers scattered all over, and a big beige stain has ruined the white carpet. Coffee. Mum never drank anything else. Her mug – the posh floral one I got her for her birthday – stands upright on the table.

The papers look like a report from one of Mum's cases. I gather them up, careful to make sure they're stacked in order. If Mum gets home she'll . . .

When . . . I think instead. Because Mum's going to be OK. I know she is.

There's a bunch of post by the door that must've been delivered after Mum went into hospital: some letters and a delivery card. I put them on the table too.

Next, I make my way to the kitchen.

I almost can't go inside when I see the table set for two,

and the remnants of the meal Mum was cooking laid out on the counter. My heart lurches. I should've been there. She thought I was still going to come over. Or maybe she hoped.

Some of it has been put away, like someone's tried to tidy after her, but they didn't do it properly, and the smell of herbs still lingers.

Mum's always been a messy cook; it drove Dad up the wall. He usually did all the cooking, and he could never quite handle it whenever she insisted that it was her turn. He would hover, cleaning up behind her. Dad is all about order. Mum was . . . is . . . free.

I decide to finish the tidying. When I'm done and everything looks normal again I stand and look around, feeling a little strange, like I'm trespassing.

Like in the dream.

What have I come here to do?

I think back to the man at the hospital with his tartan blanket and his books, and then stare around Mum's flat. *What shall I take in for her?*

I think of the mug on the table, but she can't exactly use it, can she?

In the end I settle for a throw she always keeps on the sofa, covered in yellow flowers, and a worn-out cushion that's shaped like a fox. That'll make her hospital room prettier, won't it?

I decide to try her bedroom next. As soon as I walk in her signature perfume envelops me. It's musky: some sort of wood, rose and maybe orange? It smells like comfort and childhood and home. But I daren't touch it. It's too special.

Instead I reach for her hand cream. Mum was always moisturizing her hands. She would offer me some every time, but I always refused.

'They make my fingers greasy,' I once moaned.

'Oh, don't be so silly!' she said, chasing me around the room. Eventually Mum caught me and slathered my palms in lotion. 'You'll thank me when you're my age and have the hands of a toddler.'

'That sounds so weird,' I said, grinning. At the time I imagined grown-up Mum walking around with tiny hands.

I still remember the way Mum laughed at that. Each note of it floated up, up, up, filling the room with joy, like birds singing on the first day of spring.

I put a pea-sized amount of hand cream on my palms, and rub it in carefully, the way Mum always does.

As I leave Mum's room I notice a photo by her bed. It's of my grandmother standing in front of a great big house. I've never met her, only seen photos. She died before I was born, but Mum used to say her soul went into my body, so it's like she's still here. Toddler Mum stands next to my grandmother, clinging to her skirt.

I'm so focused on my mother and grandmother that I barely notice the house. But when I do I almost gasp. Apart from the silver branches it looks exactly like the one in . . .

'My dream,' I say aloud.

Chapter 7

When Dad and I get to the hospital in the evening Edward waves me through right away. 'Your mum's doing well today,' he says with a smile, though I'm not exactly sure what that means. She's still in a coma after all.

When I walk into Mum's room I see it as if for the first time. Yesterday I was too focused on Mum to notice anything else. There are two other beds in the room, alongside Mum's, and the patients in them are asleep. I wonder what their stories are, what happened to them. I can hear their machines humming in unison, pumping air through their bodies like an orchestra. Then there's Mum's, just out of time with the others.

I walk over to her curtain and seeing her again sends a wave of something through me. Shock? Fear?

It's something else, something I can't quite pinpoint.

'Hello, lovely.' It's Amanda, the nurse who helped me yesterday. She's peering round the curtain now. I feel embarrassed to see her. 'How are you doing today?'

'Good, thanks.' I smile awkwardly. I can't stop thinking about how I cried in front of her. 'I . . . uh . . . brought some stuff in for Mum.' Suddenly I feel all shy again. 'Is it OK if . . .' My sentence fizzles out into nothing.

Amanda beams, peering into my bag. 'Let me help you with that.'

Instead of saying thanks like a normal person, I make an indiscernible noise that sounds a bit like a cow trying to sing.

Stop being weird, Saff.

The thing is, sometimes my brain just goes blank. It's like standing in a dark room where I try to reach for words, any words, but there's nothing there.

Amanda picks up the throw and places it over Mum's blanket, while I position the fox cushion at the top of her bed.

'Well then, you look much better today,' Amanda says when we're done, glancing in my direction. 'School went well?' She eyes up my snot-green uniform.

'Yeah!' I answer a little too enthusiastically.

She nods. 'Anyway, these are lovely!' she says, pointing at the blanket and cushion. She fluffs the cushion up and places it next to Mum's head, and speaks again before I have to think up a response.

'It'll be really good for your mum to have familiar things around her. Home comforts.' She smiles.

'Yeah,' I say again, grinning at her like a maniac.

Say something else, Saff.

But I can't. It feels weird to be making small talk with a virtual stranger across the bed of my unconscious mother.

'All right,' Amanda sings, unfazed. 'I'll leave you to it!' She pulls the curtains shut with finality, and I'm left alone with Mum again. The sudden silence is jarring.

I try to hold Mum's hand, but it's cold, like a corpse's, and I pull back. I try again. I wrap my fingers round hers, avoiding the tube protruding from her wrist that is keeping her body nourished. I want to warm her skin. I want her to feel my touch.

I reach into my bag and pull out Mum's hand cream. I put a little in my palms and rub them together. Then I rub it on her hands, one at a time. When I'm done I look up at Mum again. I imagine her brown eyes creasing up as she smiles, sparkling with life. I want to see them now. I want her to look at me. Even if it is one of her angry looks. Right now I'd take anything.

Open your eyes, Mum. 'Open your eyes.' I say it aloud without meaning to and cover my mouth with my hand, the other still clinging to hers, my grip firm, desperate. 'Please,' I add quietly.

She doesn't of course, because Mum's always been stubborn.

I notice the perfume still lingering on her skin. It wafts towards me as the heater blasts it in my direction.

I lean over to cover Mum with the flower-covered throw. The smell is overpowering now; I close my eyes and take it in. But my legs start to wobble, and I almost fall into the chair.

When I next open my eyes I'm back in front of the house again.

It's night-time. The stars wave hello, like they've been expecting me.

The door of the house is wide open, like it expects me too. I'm certain it's the one from the photo. Does that mean I'm in Kuwait? As soon as I think it I know I'm right.

I look to my left, where the great big iron gates stand, and to the right where an old set of swings sway in the warm breeze, and finally back at the house again.

It stands there, like the ruined palace from *Fairy Hunters*, where you collect your quests. And this time I go inside.

A tunnel of green greets me as I step through the door. Plants hang from the ceiling, their leaves skating down the walls and on to the purple-and-pink marbled floor. I sweep my hand along the wall, gathering leaves. As I pass through I think of Mum growing up here in this house. I think of her as a little child, holding on to her mother's skirt like she did in that photo. I want to swoop her up in my arms and tell her everything is going to be OK. Because that's what I need someone to tell me.

Soon I find myself in a foyer with a round table in the middle of it. Windows line one entire side of the wall, their blinds, like the house's eyelids, are pulled down, like it's asleep. The pearlescent walls sparkle in the light, and an enormous canvas of the sky stands at the furthest end of the room. This is how I imagine the fairy palace would have looked before it turned to ruin. Red and gold furniture, rich colours and patterned curtains. It's like stepping into a dream.

As I walk across the room it's as if I can feel the house breathe beneath my feet.

Whish, whoosh. Pause. Whish, whoosh. Pause. Its steady heartbeat drumming through the floors.

Another leaf-lined hallway leads to a different part of the house, and a staircase winds upwards just next to it.

I'm about to try the other rooms, to explore more, when I see it.

A bracelet.

It's the only thing on the glass-topped table, and it sparkles and glints at me.

Like it *wants* me to pick it up. In *Fairy Hunters* you always know when to collect objects, because they glow just a little brighter than everything else. That's what this reminds me of.

I see something inscribed on the bracelet, but it's in Arabic. Mum taught me it when I was younger, though we haven't had lessons in a while. I understand Arabic much better than I can read it. Mum eventually gave up trying to teach me all the letters and how to join them together, but I think I can still read some of them.

I pick the bracelet up and try to make out what it says. Slowly.

I get as far as 'am' before I hear it.

Laughter. Coming from the front door.

Then I see it. Something shoots across the room, like a star.

I realize it's a young girl, followed by another.

They pass by me so quickly I don't see their faces – just a blur of long curly hair as they bolt up the stairs.

I jump and drop the bracelet, my heart pounding.

It clatters on the table, startling me.

When I next look up I'm back at the hospital by Mum's bedside. My glasses have fallen from my face and on to the floor while I was sleeping.

As I put them on and look around the same thing happens as before.

The heat.

The sand.

Except this time, instead of silver branches I see leaves everywhere, crawling up Mum's bed, reaching for her.

I rub my eyes and after that they're gone. I wave my hand in front of my face like before and it blurs, making me feel dizzy.

I wait until the feeling passes, and then I rush out of the room without saying goodbye.

Another strange dream, I think.

Those girls . . . The curly hair. It can't be, can it?

Then I wonder, almost hope, *will it happen again?*

Chapter 8

I remember the day Mum and Dad told me they were splitting up. Mum had collected me from school; it was the afternoon we broke up for the Easter holidays. She wasn't very talkative during the walk. Usually she was always full of stories and chatter. I never understood how one person could have so much to say, especially as I've always been bad at conversation. I could never articulate how my days at school went, and I could tell that Mum found my one-word answers frustrating. We would play this game over dinner where she would ask me questions that got more and more specific. I used to call it Sherlock Investigates, although Mum never knew that.

'How was school today, Saff?'

'Fine.'

'Did you get any English homework?'

'Yes.'

'What do you have to do?'

'Write a poem.'

'What kind of poem?'

And by this point she will have cracked it. I'd end up talking through the lesson and everything I'd learned. Just when I thought it was over, Mum would ask me about another subject, and the process would start all over again.

By the end of the meal we'd both be exhausted. Mum from having to think up all the questions, and me from wondering how to answer them well enough for her to leave me alone.

Dad would usually pipe up with random observations that would have nothing to do with our conversation.

'Did you know that peanuts are actually a legume?' he would say.

Then Mum would take one look at me and smile, and we'd burst out laughing.

'What?' Dad would ask. 'What's funny?'

But that night was different.

Mum and Dad ordered a pizza. They said it was to celebrate the school holidays.

'But it's only Easter,' I said, confused. 'We never even celebrate the summer holidays.' That's when I turned to Dad and eyed him up suspiciously. 'You hate holidays!' I pointed at him accusingly. 'They're bad for work. You *always* say that.'

Dad's mouth dropped open and he gaped at me like a fish. He made a strange noise that seemed to come from somewhere between his throat and nose, before falling silent.

I automatically looked at Mum to fill in the gap, but she didn't. That's when I knew something was wrong.

'What is it?' I finally asked. 'Did my teachers say something bad about me?'

Suddenly it was like I was Sherlock, asking all the questions.

'Safiya, your dad and I have something to tell you,' Mum said. She took a deep breath, as if she was sucking in the words from the air, ready to spit them out. 'We're getting a divorce.'

I didn't look at either of them. My eyes were locked on my slice of pepperoni and sweetcorn pizza, the cheese congealed into lumps as it cooled, oil dripping on to the plate.

I counted the number of drops. One, two, three . . . four.

'Well?' Mum asked nervously.

I blinked. 'What?'

'Don't you have anything to say?' she snapped, before biting her lip. 'Sorry . . . No, it's fine, you don't need to say anything.' But I could tell she wanted me to. Mum didn't leave conversations hanging.

I looked at Dad. He was staring at his plate too, and

I could tell he was crying. Did he even want a divorce? Dad adored Mum. He was always doing little things like leaving her notes, bringing her coffee in bed, or buying her books randomly. Why would you do that and then leave someone? I was convinced Mum was behind it all.

I knew I had to say something. I could've asked why, or when, or if there was a chance they might change their minds. Instead my nine-year-old self asked, 'Can I live with Dad?'

I actually made it through a whole day of school today.

Luckily Dad never found out that I snuck off to Mum's flat the other day after lunch. When he asked where the blankets and cushions came from, I just said I picked them up one day after school.

Elle, Abir, Izzy and I just finished our lesson with Ms Belgrave. She didn't sneak me any sweets this time. It's OK, though, because as soon as we're out of the school gates Izzy pulls out a whole packet of biscuits.

'My favourite. I love you!' Abir says, taking a handful.

Izzy rolls her eyes, but grins and offers them to me.

'Thanks,' I say, taking a few too.

I can't help but notice how Abir and Elle are now whispering together in front of us, while me and Izzy lag behind. *What are they talking about?*

They suggested we head over to the bike shed today, even though I'm the only one who actually cycles to school, but they never said *why*. Suddenly I'm feeling all suspicious.

'Want one, Elle?' Izzy asks, holding them out to her.

Elle turns and pulls a face. 'I'm OK, thanks. Don't want to have crumbs all over my mouth,' she giggles.

Abir giggles too, but I don't understand the joke.

I turn to Izzy and frown. She shrugs and stuffs a biscuit in her mouth whole.

I've only been friends with Izzy and Abir since the start of the school year, so I'm still not sure how to act around them without Elle's guidance. I'm not sure Abir likes me much at all, as she always seems to be confused by the things I say or do. But Izzy's really nice when she's not following Abir around.

I notice Izzy's wearing a copper bracelet with a mermaid trinket on her wrist. It reminds me a bit of the bracelet from the house in my dream.

As soon as I picked it up the two girls appeared, like I'd pressed play on a film. And it's strange that I've dreamed about the house each time I've visited Mum. I never remember falling asleep during the visits. It just . . . sort of . . . happens.

I want to see more of the two girls. I don't recognize the first one, I've never seen her before. But the second one seems familiar with her wild curly hair . . .

'Saff?' Izzy says, holding out another biscuit.

I grin. 'Oh, sorry! Thanks.' I want to tell Izzy her bracelet is pretty, and ask her why it's a mermaid. I want to ask her what her favourite biscuits are, and what she thinks she's going to do for our English homework, but it's like my brain isn't actually wired to my mouth.

Come on, Saff, say something.

Luckily Elle saves me by calling us all over to look at a funny video of a sloth on her phone. I get the prime spot next to her, like always. Sometimes I wonder why Elle picked me, awkward Saff, when she could be best mates with anyone. It makes me feel special.

But when we get to the bike shed Elle starts to act strange. She keeps glancing around like she's expecting someone, and applies lip balm about a million times.

'What's wrong?' I ask, sitting next to her on a low wall. 'How come we're all hanging out here?' *In the cold.* Though I don't say the last bit.

Elle talks over me instead of answering my question. 'Can we play one of your mum's games?' she asks, while Izzy and Abir finish off the rest of the biscuits and chat about their weekend plans.

I think about how Mum always takes us to coffee shops and makes up conversations the people across from us could be having. She invents funny voices and stories on the spot, while me and Elle laugh so hard we usually end up spilling our drinks.

But today, because I can tell something's bothering Elle, I decide to take the lead, mimicking some of the older students who hang around in groups after school. I do different film and TV impersonations for their voices. I'm halfway through an impression of Dobby from *Harry Potter* when Elle's whole body turns stiff. Izzy and Abir, who had joined us after Elle explained the game, stop and turn.

I turn too and see a few boys from our year have approached us, including Matty Chung, the boy Elle fancies, and his best mates Jonnie and David. I whip my head towards her, but I can barely see her since she's buried her face in her hair.

'Hi, Elle.' Matty grins, and Jonnie laughs, while David nudges him.

At first I thought it was a coincidence, but now it seems like they've planned this. Especially as Elle hops off the wall and walks towards him, her face as red as her hair.

They disappear behind the bike sheds without another word.

What's going on?

'Was that an impression of Dobby?' David smiles. 'It was really good!'

I nod awkwardly. I'd hoped they hadn't heard.

David's about to say something else when Abir interrupts. 'Don't mind Saff,' she says, except she's looking at Jonnie, not David. 'She can be a bit of a weirdo.'

I look at her a little confused, because I'm pretty sure she was laughing just moments ago.

Jonnie turns to me and looks at me like I'm a piece of gum under his shoe. 'You look a bit like Dobby actually,' he says, pulling his eyelids open with his finger and thumb to make his eyes look exaggeratedly big.

His words are like a wizard's spell, and I shrink to the size of a flower.

Abir forces a giggle, like his joke was funny. David purses his lips, and Izzy frowns, but there's no Elle to stand up for me like usual.

I know now why she asked us to come here. And I know why she was whispering to Abir and acting all strange. But what I don't know is why she didn't tell me.

Suddenly I don't want to be here at all. I want Elle and me to go back to one of our houses and do homework together with a hot chocolate and snacks, instead of standing out here waiting for boys in the cold.

'I've got to go,' I mumble, so quietly I'm not sure anyone hears.

I grab my bike and pedal, pedal, pedal home.

Dad's on his computer when I get in. 'You're back a bit late,' Dad says, frowning. 'Everything OK?'

'Fine,' I say, like I always used to when Mum asked about school.

Dad lets out a sigh, and I can almost see his worries floating in the air between us, like little butterflies. I watch as they drift out of the room, and Dad turns back to his computer, satisfied with my answer. If he looked a little harder, he would see that my face is swollen from crying, my eyes blotchy and red.

I don't know why I'm crying really.

Maybe it's because Abir laughed at Jonnie's stupid joke about me looking like Dobby. Or maybe it's because my best friend is being far more grown-up than I thought we both were, and she didn't even tell me. Or maybe it's Mum.

There are a lot of maybes to consider, and right now I miss all of Mum's questions. If she were here, she would get to the bottom of things, and I would be able to figure out why I feel like there are rocks burrowing deep into my chest. But there's only Dad, and he doesn't know how to play Sherlock Investigates.

'I'm going up,' I say.

'All right, love.'

I spend the rest of the night gaming, with Lady resting at my feet. As soon as I put my headphones on all of my worries disappear, and it's like I'm transported to a different world where I don't have to worry about Mum, or friends, or being something I'm not.

Chapter 9

It takes a lot of convincing before Dad lets me go up to Mum's hospital room by myself again, especially after Amanda let it slip that I cried the first time. I wanted to be alone so I could dream about the house, but I feel stupid now. I've been here for five minutes already and nothing has happened. Maybe it was a coincidence after all . . .

But as soon as I go to stand up the shiny hospital floor is replaced by sandy concrete slabs, and when I look up I see a bright yellow sun in the sky, instead of artifical lights on a grey ceiling.

As the house materializes in front of me for the third time I know, in my heart, that something magical is happening. I rush inside, across the foyer to the gold-lined, glass-topped table, and I see it again. The bracelet. Just like before it glows slightly brighter than everything else, and I'm reminded of the crystals we have to collect in *Fairy Hunters*, which have gold halos surrounding them, letting us know they're items we can collect. I pick the bracelet up, clasp it firmly in my hands, and wait.

The same laughter, the same blur of hair. But I follow them this time. The two girls.

The house is awake today. I can feel its heartbeat pounding. The smells are more vivid with the bracelet in my hand, the colours brighter, like opening the curtains on a sunny day.

'Hello,' I call, out of breath, as I chase the girls up the stairs, crossing parts of the house I've never seen before. There are photo frames with pictures that I know hold stories, and doors that lead to rooms I'd love to see. But I don't have time to explore. Not now. The girls ignore me, intent on chasing one another. 'Hello, where am I?' I try again.

They stop suddenly in front of a set of lavish forest-green double doors, but I've built up too much momentum and I brace myself just as I'm about to crash right into them.

I close my eyes and hold my hands out.

Instead of clothes and hair, I feel wood and brass. It's as if I've walked right through the girls, and straight into the door.

Then, all of a sudden, the doors swing open with force.

I jump out of the way just as a woman appears. She has orange hair, like fire, and a beautiful face that looks like . . .

Mum? But she looks different here. That's when I picture the photo by Mum's bed, and my eyes widen in realization.

'What on earth is going on?' my grandmother demands.

'I . . . It wasn't . . .' I stutter, but the strangest thing happens. She walks straight past me. Straight *through* me.

She can't see me. I test out my theory and wave my hands in front of her face. I even try to touch her arm, but my hand goes through her. *None of them can see me.*

They always say if you cross a ghost, you feel a shiver down your spine. That's not what this is like, because I feel nothing, not even a breeze.

Maybe because *I'm* the ghost.

'Aminah, are you tormenting your sister again?' my grandmother asks, her voice like poison. 'We have guests and they can hear you from all the way out here.'

I frown. Aminah?

'I'm not, Mama, I swear,' the older girl calls from the landing.

And that's when I confirm it. The wild curly hair. That's Mum. And the younger girl must be her sister.

'Mama, she hit me!' The younger girl, my Aunt Zaina, pouts, showing off her sore arm.

Mum, or I guess Aminah, rolls her eyes. 'Zaina stole my bracelet,' she says, both of them speaking a mixture of

English and Arabic.

I look at the bracelet in my hands. It's gold with white pearl beads and an Arabic inscription.

أمينة

Aminah.

'It's here!' I say, waving it in front of their faces. But there's no point. I'm invisible to them all.

'And why would she do that?' My grandmother, 'Mama', asks, her voice as sharp as her features. 'It has your name on it.'

'Why don't you ask her?' Aminah replies, and I can't help but smile because she's just like the Mum I know.

'I didn't steal it, Mama,' Zaina insists. 'She *lost* it.'

Mama turns to Zaina now. 'Go inside and ask your aunt if she wants more tea,' she orders. Zaina nods right away. 'And close the door behind you.'

Mama turns to Aminah. 'Where are you going?'

In the time it took for Mama to address Zaina, Aminah had tried to sneak off downstairs. She spins round now like a clumsy ballerina, and faces Mama.

'Are you a child?' Mama asks.

Aminah shakes her head.

'How old are you?'

'Thirteen,' she mutters.

Like me.

'Then –' Mama pauses – 'you know it's wrong to hit your sister.'

'But, Mama, Zaina was the one who –'

Mama puts her hand up to silence Aminah, and her voice stops dead.

'Zaina is younger than you, Aminah. You can't use her as an excuse.'

'Sorry.' Aminah sniffs, and I see tears in her eyes.

'*And* you lost your bracelet.'

Aminah doesn't argue back this time.

'I won't buy you nice things any more if you can't look after them.'

Mama's not yelling, but she doesn't need to.

'Sorry, Mama,' Aminah squeaks again, eyes trained on her feet.

I don't recognize this side of Mum. She looks scared and mouse-like.

'You're back from school for one day . . . *one* day,' Mama says, her voice echoing across the hall despite her tiny frame, 'and already you cause trouble. I wish sometimes your father would take you travelling with him over the summer. Then I wouldn't have to deal with all of this.' She sighs exasperatedly. It's an offhand remark, kind of like the ones Mum makes sometimes, but I can almost feel the burn of it on Aminah's heart.

Aminah's tears fall freely now. She runs down the stairs, out of the house and into the scorching heat of the courtyard.

I follow her, barely keeping up. I want to give her the

bracelet and tell her she hasn't lost it after all.

Outside, Aminah sits on the set of swings I saw last time and lets herself cry. I try to pat her shoulder to comfort her, but my hand goes right through her.

I think for a moment about the rules in this dream in the same way I would approach one of my games. I can't touch anyone and they can't see me. But I can pick things up, like the bracelet, and brush my hands against the leaves on the walls.

I sit on the swing next to Aminah and it jiggles around, but she doesn't appear to see that either.

Aminah rocks gently to and fro, letting her feet graze the ground, until her tears dry up and she falls silent.

But the sound of someone singing cuts through the quiet.

'Hello?' Aminah calls, looking around her.

Silence.

Then: 'Ow!'

Something lands hard on Aminah's shoulders. She whips her head up to the right, searching for the source. She doesn't spot it, but I do. Just about.

Two cats rush under the shelter of one of the cars.

They had come from somewhere beyond the courtyard wall and had used Aminah as a landing pad. From down here all you can see are palm trees beyond a great big wall. They hold more of the silver branches that line the house.

The singing has stopped now, and is replaced by the

light padding of feet on sand.

'Hello?' Aminah tries again. She pulls an old slide up against the wall, climbs to the top, and peeks her head over.

I do the same, leaning through her body to look over too. For a moment it's like we're the same person.

Over the wall is a long, hidden alleyway filled with all sorts of overgrown trees, which create a tunnel-like arch across it. Each end is blocked by concrete, concealing it from the outside world. Aminah and I spot a short-haired girl just as she starts climbing the wall into the courtyard of one of the other houses.

Aminah starts to call for the girl, but her own name echoes from somewhere behind us. We turn at the same time.

Zaina struts up to the slide. 'You got in trouble!' she teases, Aminah's bracelet dangling from her wrist. I look down at my right hand, but the bracelet is gone.

Aminah sighs and looks back, but the girl has disappeared.

And in that moment everything else disappears too. The house, the courtyard, Aminah and her sister.

And suddenly, instead of the slide, I'm sitting on the hospital chair next to Mum's bed, her hair as curly and as wild as it was when she was thirteen.

Chapter 10

'How was your mum?' Dad asks as I get into the car. Lady's in the back seat and she dives into the front to say hello by licking one of my knees. 'The doctors didn't have much to report this time.'

'Fine,' I say, stroking Lady until she settles into the footwell, my mind swirling with thoughts of Mum and her family, and the dreams. I spent way longer in the dream this time, but when I woke up only a few minutes had passed. Kind of like in Narnia, when Lucy goes through the wardrobe during a game of hide-and-seek. She's gone for ages and ages, but when she gets back they're still playing.

'Did you speak to her?' Dad asks as we pull out of the car park.

'Who? Mum?' I look up, a little alarmed. *Is he testing me?*

Does he know?

Dad raises his eyebrows. 'No, the Queen,' he says, smirking at his own joke, and I realize obviously he doesn't.

'Not really . . .' I say, not sure how to explain that I usually spend the whole visit asleep. 'Should I?' I turn to him, my brown eyes meeting his blue.

Dad shrugs. 'I was just doing some reading about –' he hesitates, and I know he doesn't want to say the word 'coma' – 'patients, and how you can help them recover.' He explains everything he's read to me.

I try to listen, but my mind is far, far away. In Kuwait.

I check the temperature in Dad's car and see it's almost freezing outside. I find it hard to believe that moments ago I could *feel* the warmth. Smell it. It smelled just like Mum's perfume.

Three visits to Mum, three times I've had these strange dreams. Except, these aren't like any dreams I've had before. Usually my dreams are hazy, and what happens in them is random. These are different . . . They play out like a story. But how are they happening, and why?

Then it hits me.

'Dad?' I bark, making him jump.

He turns to me, eyebrows creased.

'Is it OK if we stop by Mum's flat, just for a minute?'

A pause.

'Of course,' Dad says, and his voice is softer than I've heard it in years.

It sounds like it did that time school called up to say I had fallen over and broken my two front teeth. Dad came rushing in, wrapped me up in his arms, and told me how brave I was.

A while later I jump out of the car. 'I won't be long,' I promise.

Back in Mum's flat I'm seeing things I've never noticed before, like everything has a gold halo around it. The table in her hallway looks just like the one that held the bracelet in the dream, the photos on the walls do as well, and the plants that make her flat feel alive. They're real, all of them.

So, what if the dreams are real too?

As I approach Mum's bedroom door her perfume beckons me in. I follow it like Alice followed the rabbit to Wonderland.

I walk over to the dressing table, open Mum's jewellery drawer, and find it packed with beautiful shining gems. Earrings, bracelets, necklaces. It's like finding loot in a game. Except there's only one thing I need.

When I see it, tucked away at the back, like it hasn't been worn for years, my legs start to wobble. It feels like a butterfly is lodged in my throat, fluttering from my chest right up to my oesophagus. It's real. Mum's bracelet is real.

I reach out for it, feeling the smooth gold, tracing my fingers over her name.

أمينة

Aminah.

It's exactly as it looked in the dream. But the thing is, I've never seen this bracelet before in real life.

Chapter 11

The house is quieter today, like a forest after rainfall. I walk up to the glass table, just as I did last time, but the bracelet is no longer there. Instead it's dangling from my wrist after I put it on in Mum's flat.

It makes me feel closer to her somehow, and braver too. Like the bracelet is my armour, and I'm ready to go into battle.

A familiar smell draws me to the kitchen. I walk across the marble-floored foyer, bypassing the stairs, and enter another leafy tunnel.

I know this house is Mum's childhood home but it feels different, more like it's a living creature rather than just a house. The heartbeat follows me as I walk, drumming to my steps. When I enter the kitchen I'm met with the biggest feast I've seen in my life. I recognize some of it from dishes Mum's cooked before.

Stuffed vine leaves, *zaatar* bread and cheese, stacks of sugar sweets and honeysuckle melon, and lots and lots of tea. I peer around to see if I can find the person who made all this food, but no one is there, and I hear nothing but the pulse of the house, and the thump, thump, thumping in my chest.

I sit down, reach for a stuffed vine leaf, and take a bite. It's delicious.

I take another, and pour myself a helping of tea too. I bite into a sugar sweet when I'm done, the syrup dripping down my chin. I catch it with my thumb and lick each of my fingers in delight. A few minutes, maybe more, pass, until I'm interrupted by a very determined miaow.

I jump, and my cup of tea clatters to the floor. But when I look back it's on the table again, where I first found it.

Sitting in front of me, its tail wagging impatiently, is a cat with yellow eyes.

I stand up and walk towards it. As soon as I take my first step it launches itself at the back door, which stands open, and walks a few paces into the courtyard beyond.

Then it sits, looking at me determinedly again. And it glows a little brighter than everything else, the way the bracelet did. I think I'm supposed to follow it.

The cat is a grey tabby; bits of its fur are missing in

places, and there's a scar on its left ear. It looks like a stray. But the most remarkable thing about the cat is the white heart-shaped line of fur that starts in the middle of its back and winds down towards its tail.

As we make our way along the courtyard I notice the house is crumbling in places it wasn't before. One of the windows has no glass in it any more, and I can see the staircase peeking through a great big gouge in the wall. I have to dodge pieces of rubble the way I do in *Fairy Hunters* whenever I approach the ruined palace.

I'm back at the swings now, the ones Aminah sat on the day she was crying. That's when I realize this must be one of the cats that had landed on her head. I didn't see them properly last time, but I know there were two of them.

'Where's your friend?' I ask.

The cat doesn't answer.

'Just like Lady,' I mutter.

The cat jumps up on to the courtyard wall, looks at me, and miaows again.

This time I *know* it wants me to follow because the slide is standing there in the same spot as before. I rest my hand on one of the silver branches as I climb and notice a flower has bloomed where Aminah stood. It's bright yellow, with a little cupped section in the middle and five long petals closing round it protectively.

As soon as my feet hit the sandy ground on the other side of the wall I hear a voice.

'What are you, some sort of assassin? I didn't hear you at all.'

The girl from beyond the wall is staring at me now.

I soon realize it's not me she's looking at but Aminah, who is standing right next to me.

It was morning when I last had one of these dreams, but this time the sun is beginning to set.

Aminah laughs. 'Maybe,' she retorts. 'I was beginning to think I'd imagined you.'

The girl looks at her quizzically.

'From the other day?' Aminah continues. She seems a little embarrassed. 'I called out to you as you were climbing back over . . .' She lets her words fizzle out.

The girl's eyes widen. 'It was you? I've been avoiding this place because I thought some stupid little kid started playing here.'

The pair settle beneath a tree, and I join them. From down here the wall that leads back to Aminah's house looks giant, like a skyscraper, and the trees just as tall. I can no longer see either end of it. Instead I'm surrounded by a canopy of leaves and sand, like being marooned on some sort of desert island.

Everything here is strange, ever-changing. Before Aminah and the girl appeared it was just a plain old wall with some sand on the ground. Now it's like a secret garden. Suddenly I feel so tiny, in a big, big world, the way I always do when I play *Fairy Hunters*.

One minute you're casting spells against a wizard, the next you're hit with a shrink potion and you're the size of a mouse. And, all of a sudden, your perspective shifts.

The cat I had followed sits a few metres away next to a smaller cat that looks identical. But even they're different here. Bigger, wilder.

Aminah scowls. 'I'm not a child! It was probably my sister you heard.'

'So, what's your speciality?' the girl asks, changing the subject at lightning speed.

Aminah frowns. 'What?'

'You know, if you're an assassin?'

The sun's almost gone now, and the girl pulls a torch from her backpack, setting it out between us all. It lights up the circle like a magic orb, but everything surrounding us is coated in inky darkness – apart from the two pairs of feline eyes that stare from the bushes.

'Oh, yes, right!' Aminah says, biting her lip, as if in contemplation.

'Mine's a bow and arrow,' the girl says, answering her own question. 'That way I can watch my victims from a distance.'

'Remind me never to come back here before you do, so you can't ambush me.'

'Who says you're allowed back?'

Aminah raises her eyebrows. 'It's behind *my* house, isn't it?'

'Mine too,' the girl says dismissively, pointing at her own home. You can just about see the top of the roof from here; it looks like a castle turret. 'And anyway, I found it first.'

'What *is* this place?' Aminah looks around in wonder the way I had moments before.

'A secret,' the girl says simply. Then she adds with a smile, 'I'll let you back if you pass the test.'

Aminah sits up straighter. 'I'm good at tests,' she says a little smugly.

I laugh. Mum's ridiculously clever.

The girl rolls her eyes. 'Not *that* kind of test.' She nods over at the cats. 'If you can pet one of them, you can come back.'

'And if I don't?'

'Then this was all a dream,' the girl whispers spookily, holding the torch up to her face.

Aminah gulps. 'Fine,' she finally says. 'I'll do it.'

Aminah stands up, her shoes noisily grazing against the ground. Immediately one pair of eyes disappears as the first cat bolts.

The girl lets out a low murmur. 'Not a good start,' she teases, the smile evident in her voice.

'Pass me the torch,' Aminah says, gritting her teeth. She holds it under her arm, takes her shoes off one at a time, and creeps silently across the sand.

I follow her, careful to be quiet too.

The second cat, the smaller of the two, is much braver.

It's poised, ready to run, but it looks curious too, eyes locked on Aminah as she inches closer and closer.

She's now less than a metre away and the cat takes a couple of steps back.

Aminah changes tack. She sits down. As soon as she does the cat stops, watching her.

'What are you doing?' the girl calls.

'Shhhh!' Aminah says, but the noise has scared the cat even more, and it bolts into the leaves after its mother.

'You lose,' the girl says coolly.

My heart sinks. I wanted her to win.

But Aminah's not given up yet. She ignores the girl and focuses instead on her task. She watches the cats peer out at her from the bushes.

She takes the torch and shines it just in front of where the cats are sitting. She darts the light left to right.

A minute passes.

Two.

Nothing.

Then, a tiny paw.

Both of the cats jump out of the bush to chase the light.

Aminah holds the torch over her head and directs it closer and closer to her until the cats are playing less than a metre away. She clicks her tongue. Both cats look up at her, alarmed, as if surprised to see her there. Then Aminah puts her left hand out, palm up, beneath the cats' mouths. They sniff. And she takes her chance.

She strokes the smaller cat – the braver one – first. It pulls back a little, until it realizes she isn't going to hurt it. And then, rather abruptly, it leans into her, purring.

The second cat lets her pet it once, before retreating back into the bushes.

Aminah turns and points the torch at the girl. 'I win!' she says triumphantly. She settles back into her old spot and puts her shoes back on.

'I was kind of joking, you know,' the girl admits. 'Even I've never been near those cats. I've decided what your speciality is, by the way.'

'What?'

'Cat herder.'

Aminah laughs. 'That can be my nickname, but my real name is Aminah.'

'Mine's Rawan.' The girl smiles. 'Meet at the same time tomorrow, OK?'

Aminah nods.

'And next time, bring snacks,' Rawan orders as she climbs over the wall and heads back home. As soon as she's gone the night falls silent, and the inky darkness covers me and Aminah like a blanket.

Chapter 12

The more I think about the dreams, the more I understand what's going on. They're all happening in Kuwait, in Mum's old house. And they're happening in the past. I know this because Mum's my age in them. But I only have these dreams in the hospital when I visit Mum. Recently, when I've been going to bed at night, my brain is like a blank canvas, like it saves up all its energy for the visits. But there's more to it, I think, because these dreams might actually be real.

The bracelet glowed, and so did the cats. And when I picked up the bracelet and followed the cats it unlocked something in the dream. It reminds me a little of a cutscene in a game, where you watch something that tells you what your next mission will be. But the thing about games is they have a bigger purpose, like saving the world. I just need to figure out what that is. And the only way to do that is to keep dreaming!

'You sure you don't want me to come inside?' Dad asks, frowning. 'You're not . . . nervous, or lonely?'

It must be weird for Dad to see me do this alone. When I was a bit younger I used to freak out if he left the room for too long. I suppose he can't pair that Safiya with this one. I'm not sure I can either.

I shake my head. 'No!' I say a little too quickly.

I don't know how to explain that I'm not lonely at all, not when I'm exploring the house or watching Aminah.

'I like it,' I add. 'Being alone with Mum.' It's half true. I do like it, but I'm not exactly *alone*.

Dad stares at me, long and hard, and then he nods. 'I'll just nip and do the food shop and then pick you up. OK?'

'Perfect!' I sing.

Dad's a bit more worried than usual since the doctors and nurses were acting strangely when we got to the hospital today. They said words like 'slow progress' and 'monitoring' in hushed whispers to Dad.

Could that be why the house was crumbling?

I'm trying not to think about that side of things too much. I've got enough to focus on.

I follow the familiar path up to Mum's ward. Everything around me smells like lemon, so strong it's almost sickly. When I get to Mum's room I take my usual seat by her bed. I lay my head next to her arm, just as I have done before. I shut my eyes and wait for sleep to take me.

I wait.

And wait.

After several minutes I sit up again. *What's wrong?*

Everything is the same as it has been. So, why am I not falling asleep?

That's when I panic.

I stand up and pace around, not sure what to do with myself. I leave the room and walk back in to start the ritual again, but nothing works.

'Safiya!' Amanda calls as she walks in.

Please go away, I think, *so I can see my mum.*

'Hello,' I say instead, not doing a very good job of sounding enthusiastic.

Elle's always really good at this sort of thing, but not me. Thinking of Elle makes me feel like bitter medicine is seeping down my throat. All she talked about at school the day after we went to the bike shed was kissing Matty. But she never explained why she didn't tell me, her best friend, about it first.

We've been plodding along this week like normal, but something feels a little . . . off. We don't send each other as many messages as we used to; Elle just chats to the whole group instead, like I'm not enough any more.

'How are you holding up?' Amanda asks me, glancing at Mum briefly with a frown on her face.

Usually Amanda's really cheerful, so this sudden change

worries me.

Is it to do with what the doctors were saying? It can't be all that bad, can it? Mum's only been in hospital a couple of weeks. I once had the flu for that long, and had to stay off school for ages.

But then Amanda turns back to me, all smiles again. 'You know, we've had loads of people visit your mum.' She leans forward, whispering conspiratorially. 'She's our most popular patient on the ward!'

That's when I notice them. All the cards lined up on the window next to Mum's bed, from people's she's helped, friends from work and the pottery class she sometimes goes to. Amanda squeezes in next to me to show me them, like it'll make me feel better. Like it doesn't remind me that Mum seemed to be able to get along with everyone but me.

I get a whiff of hospital-standard lemon-scented soap as Amanda leans over me to show me each card. It's so strong that it makes me feel ill, but everyone here smells of it.

'Great,' I say flatly. *Say something else, Saff.*

But I can't think straight, because I'm too busy imagining Amanda and all the other hospital staff dressed up in giant lemon costumes.

'Anyway,' Amanda continues, 'I've been meaning to ask, since you were thoughtful enough to bring in your mum's blanket and cushion, does she have a favourite shampoo? I know it's an odd question, but I've been washing her hair this week and I noticed it smelled so lovely when she came in . . . much nicer than the shampoo we have here . . . and it lasted for so long too! Like magic. I wondered whether you would prefer we use that instead? It's common among our patients . . .' She goes on for a while and for some reason alarm bells start ringing in my mind because she seems so . . . concerned.

'Are you worried about Mum?' I ask seriously.

Amanda pauses, and then she paints a smile on her face in the brightest colours. 'I think it's good for us all to do everything we can to aid your mum's recovery. Familiar sounds and smells, in particular, can be helpful. Which is why . . .'

I don't listen to the rest of her sentence because I know what she means. She wants us to do what we can to help Mum *wake up*.

I think, for a moment, about Amanda's words.

Sounds and smells.

All of a sudden something in my mind clicks. And that's when I know what's missing, because I noticed it every other time I had one of the strange dreams.

I glance at the clock. Dad won't be any longer than half an hour, maybe forty-five minutes at most.

'Going already?' Amanda asks as I stand.

'I'll be back,' I answer, finally smiling at her.

She blinks in surprise. I suppose you would if you'd been talking to a girl who barely said a word for about ten minutes and then suddenly started grinning at you like a maniac.

Back at Mum's flat I rush to her bedroom and straight
for the perfume bottle. It's purple with glass cut like a
diamond, and a heart-shaped gold stopper.

Something happens as soon as I pick it up. A flash of
colour.

I apply the perfume to my wrist and rub my forearms
together. The smell wafts upwards and forms a cloud. In it
I can just about see Aminah and Rawan, the girl from the
secret hideaway, chatting together.

But then, like an old memory I'm straining to remember,
it fizzles out and I'm left alone in Mum's bedroom.

I check the clock – half an hour left – and slip the
perfume into my bag.

When I get to the hospital for the second time today, there's
a different nurse on duty, and she pretty much ignores me,
which is a relief; I don't have much time.

I pull the curtains shut and begin the ritual.

Mum's body is laid flat, hands by her sides. Her hair is
fanned out and wild like some sort of earth fairy.

I smooth out her bed covers and pull a few strands of
hair away from her face, for no particular reason other than
it feels right.

Then I pull the perfume from my pocket and untwist
the stopper. I gather some of the musk in the little pipette
and place a drop on either side of Mum's ears, then a third

on her neck.

I watch it slide down her throat and sink, sink, sink into her skin.

I notice the woody smell first, then the rose – each note of the perfume floats towards me like dandelion seeds in springtime – and finally the orange. It completes the scent like ingredients in a potion.

This time the transition is more intense, maybe because the perfume is fresh.

I can feel grains of sand in my mouth. I can taste Kuwait. The room starts to disappear before my eyes, and the beeping of the monitor next to Mum's bed stops. Instead I hear Aminah's voice as if she was next to me now.

And above it all I can feel a surge, like an electric shock, as it travels from Mum's body to mine. But I'm not quite sure what it is. Magic?

Chapter 13

'What are you, some sort of assassin? I didn't hear you at all.'

My heart sinks at the familiar words. This is what happened last time. But I suppose I should have expected that as I'd followed the cat again.

I watch the scene play out for a few seconds before I decide to go back inside and try another room.

Maybe then I'll see something new.

I cross the courtyard again and retrace my steps back to the kitchen. It looks different today, more worn. There are cracks in the walls and floor that stretch through the hall and up the stairs. Some of the ceiling has crumbled in places, leaving chunks of cement everywhere.

The heartbeat is much fainter too, and I just know it's to do with what the doctors said.

I'm worried that the house will turn to dust before I have the chance to understand what is happening.

Out of nowhere wisps of smoke appear above my head. I blink once, twice, and wonder whether my eyes are playing tricks on me. On my third blink the smoke takes shape. A bird swoops down and round my face, its wings fluttering delicately. I twirl round and round, and follow it. I hold my hand out and try to touch it, but every time I do it flies just out of reach.

Soon I'm facing the staircase again. I breathe in the bird's smoky scent, and I'm reminded of Mum. Every so often she would pull out this wooden pot shaped like a bird, and light tiny pieces of coal in its open beak. She called it *bakhoor*, and explained to me that her mum did the same when she was young to cleanse the room of old smells. But I know Mum did it mostly when she was stressed, as if she wanted to smoke away the bad feelings too.

She would walk round and round the house, and, after that, her flat – the smoke trailing behind her like a ghost.

Today I follow the smoke up the winding staircase, bypassing the living room on the first floor, where I first met Aminah, Zaina and Mama. I peek through some of the doors, which lead to bathrooms and bedrooms, but something tells me they're not where I'm supposed to be going, because the smoke keeps flying up.

At the very top of the house the smoke stops in front of a closed door.

I realize the gentle drumming of the house is louder here, like this is where its heart lies.

I wrap my fingers round the cool metal of the doorknob. I twist, and twist, but it doesn't budge. I frown and try again.

Odd. Why is this door locked?

There's a large crack in it, and the wood has splintered in places, like the walls that are crumbling in the kitchen and the photos that hang faded on the walls. I peer through the crack and find a world of bright blue and purple. There's a great big wardrobe, clothes spilling out of it, at one end, and an old-school television at the other. That's when I realize it's another bedroom.

At the centre of the room is a small wooden bed. And sleeping in the bed is a woman. It takes me a few seconds to realize it's Mum. I can tell by her wild hair. But it's not thirteen-year-old Aminah this time, it's actual grown-up Mum.

My heart flips and twirls and dances like a leaf in the wind. I gasp and step back, leaning against the banister to hold myself up.

The smoke twirls me round, spinning me away from the door, before trailing down the stairs.

I watch it go for a moment, before turning back and peering through the door again. As I put my hands up to the door the drumming feels louder, more desperate, like it's willing me to go inside. Or is it warning me?

Without realizing it I call for her. 'Mum?' I say. 'Mum, wake up!'

But she doesn't move.

I try the door again, but it doesn't budge.

But before I can try it once more, the house starts to fade as I'm pulled back to the hospital. First the roof, then the walls, and finally the floor.

I feel my world start to crumble and I scream as I tumble down, down down, like Alice when she falls into the rabbit hole.

Chapter 14

A key.

That's what I need to unlock the door to Mum's room. I realize now that's the purpose of these dreams, to get into that room.

I still don't know what the cutscenes have to do with it all. And why did the dream make me watch the second cutscene again? Usually that only happens if you haven't completed your mission. Maybe my mission is to unlock the door, and after that it'll unlock the next cutscene and I can carry on visiting Aminah.

'Your turn,' Izzy says, interrupting my thoughts.

Izzy's brought some make-up into school to try on each of us. We're spending our lunch break hiding behind the stage in the hall – where the heaters are on full blast – playing with eyeshadow.

We've all picked our own colour, like we're in a girl band. Mine's purple.

I smile back at Izzy and crawl over to where she's sitting. 'Are you going to be brave?' she asks, like a parent chastising a child. I refused to do it earlier until Izzy reminded me we would take it straight off for lessons.

'Yes, Mum,' I respond without thinking.

Izzy's eyes widen, probably because she's thinking about *my* mum.

'Oops,' I add a beat later, wondering if I've just said something really inappropriate.

I laugh nervously, and Izzy laughs with me, so I know it's not awkward. Then she asks about Mum.

Elle hasn't asked me about her recently, not since she started seeing Matty officially. They announced it online and the whole year commented on it like they were celebrities.

I tell Izzy about the hospital visits and how I've been going to Mum's flat. The doctors gave us some good news this morning. Mum twitched her hand in the middle of the night while the nurse was checking up on her. They think it might have happened quite a few times over the last couple of days. Apparently that's a sign that she's getting better!

'That's amazing, Saff!' Izzy says, hugging me, her long hair tickling my face. She always ties it up at school. Last year some of the boys used to pull off her hair bobble and throw it in the bin. Izzy never said anything, just quietly pulled another one out of her bag and tied her hair back up like it never happened. Eventually they gave up and picked on someone else, probably because that kind of thing doesn't seem to bother Izzy.

When I pull away I notice Elle glance at us and I wonder, hope, that she's a little jealous. When we're done talking I feel lighter. Holding everything in feels like carrying a heavy backpack to school, but instead of books and stationery, it's spilling with secrets and updates on Mum's condition. I haven't told anyone about the house, though, and I don't plan to.

'OK,' Izzy says when we're done talking. 'Now sit still, or I'll make you look like you have a black eye.'

A few minutes later Elle calls for me across the stage. 'You look so pretty, Saff!' she says.

My chest swells with pride. It's nice to have my best friend notice me. It feels a bit like the old days. Sort of.

'She's right, Saff, that colour suits you so much!' Abir adds, which is uncharacteristically kind of her. I make an effort to smile at her and try to forget that she laughed at Jonnie's joke when we went to the bike shed. Maybe I can move past it. Somehow.

'Let's have a look,' I say, bouncing up and down. I'm sitting on my knees on the floor while Izzy sits cross-legged in front of me.

'Not yet!' she scolds. 'You're only allowed to see when it's finished.'

After a moment Elle and Abir get distracted by something on their phones and the room falls silent. I'm suddenly very aware of how close Izzy is to my face, and it's making me feel insecure.

I wonder if she notices the little dents in my cheeks from popping spots, my wonky eyebrows, or my frog-like eyes. Is she judging me? Collecting my insecurities only to throw them back at me like Jonnie did the other day?

But Izzy frowned at him, didn't she? She didn't laugh the way Abir did.

'Do you want to do this sort of thing when you grow up?' I ask, if only to distract myself from the bad thoughts.

Izzy looks into my eyes for a second. 'No. I mean, I enjoy doing it, but I prefer drawing.'

'What kind of things? Like, pirate ships or apples?'

Izzy laughs. 'Um . . . characters.' She almost whispers it. I have a feeling it's because she doesn't want the others to hear. 'I didn't really have any friends when I joined secondary school, so I just . . . drew them. Stupid, huh?'

I feel something flutter in my chest. I was so busy being protective of Elle that I never thought about what it would be like *not* to have a best friend.

'I don't think that's stupid at all!' I say passionately. 'Can I see them?' But Izzy doesn't respond, and I worry I've put her on the spot. So, I try a different question. 'Have you ever watched any of the Studio Ghibli films? The animation is made up of these *amazing* illustrations. If you like drawing, you'll love the films.'

Izzy shakes her head, but she seems interested.

My eyes widen. 'You *have* to!' I go on for a while about all my favourites. Izzy picks the one she thinks sounds best, *Kiki's Delivery Service*, and promises to watch it over half term.

'Anyway,' Izzy says, spurred on by our chat, 'I'm not sure if I want to draw or be a vet.'

'That's cool too,' I say. 'I love animals, but I can't ever imagine doing operations on them or anything like that.'

Izzy nods sagely. 'It would be hard, but I'm not very squeamish. You can't be when you have two younger sisters.'

I nod, wondering what it would be like to have sisters or brothers. I can't help but think of Aunt Zaina, who lives in Kuwait. Dad rang her the other day to tell her about Mum. I wasn't there, but apparently she was quite upset. Dad said I can chat to her when he rings to update her next week. I'll probably chicken out, though. I'm not very good at speaking on the phone.

'I don't have any siblings,' I say. 'But I do have a dog!'

Izzy's face lights up like a starry night. 'I can't believe I didn't know that! What's its name?'

'Lady!' I say, and then I talk about her for ages. I tell Izzy about the way she follows me around the house, how she always knows the best way to cheer me up. I tell her how moody she can be, but how that makes me love her even more.

As I talk I feel a warmth spread through my body.

Maybe I don't have to have just *one* friend. Maybe there's room for someone else after all.

'Done!' Izzy declares eventually, handing me a compact mirror.

I look at myself and almost gasp. I love it. The purple makes my brown eyes sparkle, especially with the mascara Izzy added. I've never tried it before but my eyelashes are like giant spider legs. In a good way.

I frown.

'What's wrong?' Izzy looks worried.

I pout. 'I don't want to take it off for lessons.'

Izzy's face relaxes.

'You're really good,' I add. 'Have you thought of going into animal grooming? Bit of lipstick for the poodle, some eyelashes for the daschund?'

Izzy laughs so loudly she snorts. 'Would you like your eyeliner in a cat-flick style, Ms Collie?' she says in an overly posh voice.

'Oh, I couldn't possibly! Can't stand cats,' I retort, and we fall into a fit of giggles.

She takes her green eyeshadow off and leaves a few minutes later to chat to one of our teachers before lessons start. I slide back towards the wall, lean against the radiator and let the warmth permeate through my body. I'm just about finished removing my make-up, when something weird happens.

I can smell it. Mum's perfume.

I sit up and look around. I half expect Mum to jump out from behind the curtain and yell, 'Surprise!' Then she'll tell me that she's cured and that she loves me and that she's sorry about our argument.

I'll say the same and we'll go back to her flat together. I'll tell her all about the dreams and how she was like a sleeping princess waiting to be rescued from her tower.

But she doesn't.

Instead I notice her perfume in Elle's hand.

My body freezes and I count the number of drops she uses on herself and Abir. One, two, three, four, five dreams down the drain.

'Elle!' I eventually choke out.

Elle and Abir look up at me. 'What?' she asks innocently. 'It was poking out of your coat, Saff. Sorry. It's cool, though. Very vintage.'

She doesn't realize what she's doing, I say to myself, but I still stand up and snatch it back, nostrils flaring like an angry bull.

'What's your *problem?*' Abir says, rolling her eyes.

'It's my mum's.' I bend down so I'm level with her. 'And there are only a few drops left.' My voice doesn't wobble and I don't turn away. I look her right in the eye. 'Want to say something else, Abir?'

She stares at me for a moment, mouth open. Then she shakes her head.

The monster in my belly growls in satisfaction. I haven't seen it since my argument with Mum.

'Good.' The monster cheers.

I grab my things then, and storm out.

I can hear Elle and Abir whispering furiously to one another as I leave. It makes me feel uncomfortable. What if they're saying mean things about me? Part of me wants to turn round and apologize, the way the old Saff would have. But I don't.

Elle scribbles **Sorry** in her notebook, during History. She adds a smiley face underneath it.

It's fine, I write back. I leave out the smiley face, though.

When I get home from school Lady bounds up to me, acting like she hasn't seen me for days, even though it's only been a few hours.

I bend down, stroke her, and kiss her forehead.

'Want some treats?' I ask in a high-pitched voice. Lady jumps up on me and wags her tail. That's her way of saying, 'Yes.'

'Come on then!'

I walk over to the kitchen windowsill to her treats. They're in a ceramic pot shaped like two cats, with their tails curled round one another.

It's only when I go to shut the lid that I notice the resemblance. The heart-shaped marking on their backs.

Weird.

I empty Lady's treats into a container. She looks up at me, scandalized. 'I'm not stealing them!' I assure her. 'But you have to admit,' I say, 'it's pretty offensive for *dog* treats to be in a *cat* pot, isn't it?'

I give Lady two of them, because she looks kind of annoyed. She responds by slinking off into the living room and taking a nap.

After I give it a good clean I stick the pot in one of Mum's old hat boxes under my bed for safekeeping, until I can figure out exactly what is going on.

Chapter 15

'Look at this,' Matty whispers to David next to me.

'That's hilarious,' David says in a robot voice.

'Spottie Lottie,' Matty adds smugly, obviously pleased with the rhyme he's made up.

My stomach lurches. They're talking about Charlotte Baker and, by the sounds of it, what they have to say isn't very nice.

I watch them for a while unnoticed. They've basically spent our entire ICT lesson taking photos of people and laughing at them. Matty's even added little red splashes coming out of Charlotte's spots to look like lava on a volcano.

Matty catches me looking and raises his eyebrows. 'Want to have a look?' he says, shoving his phone towards me. I turn away and shake my head. 'You're in there somewhere,

Dobby.' He adds the last bit so quietly I can pretend not to have heard.

I ignore him, but I can't ignore the jolts of electricity going through my stomach.

Matty laughs in my face and crosses the room to some of the other boys, including Jonnie. I can hear a ripple of laughter rising and falling, like the notes on a glockenspiel.

David stays in his seat. I can feel his eyes on me. Eventually I turn to face him.

'I . . .' He rubs the back of his neck. He takes a breath and starts again. 'I just wanted to say, I heard about your mum and I hope . . . I hope you're OK. My dad was ill last year . . .'

He smiles awkwardly at me, like he's embarrassed.

'Really?' I ask 'I'm sorry . . .' I'm just as bad at this sort of thing as he is. 'Is he . . . OK now?'

David's face lights up. 'Yeah, he is.' He pauses. 'And your mum'll be too, I bet.'

I nod. *I hope so*, I think.

'Back to your seat, please, Matty,' Mr Mitchell says, interrupting our conversation. 'Or do you want a detention?' The room falls silent, and everyone turns to stare at Matty.

I cross my fingers, hoping he'll get in trouble.

'Sorry, sir,' Matty responds, shooting him a winning smile. 'I was just asking Jonnie a question about the work.'

'That's OK,' Mr Mitchell says, softening like butter.

'Just make sure you come to me next time.' He turns away and my jaw drops. I can't believe he fell for that!

Matty returns to his seat and shows David another one of his victims.

I feel angry, my insides burning, but on the outside all I do is freeze, because I'm a massive coward. So instead, I get revenge the only way I know how. I imagine Matty and Jonnie as wizards in *Fairy Hunters*, and I'm the most powerful fairy around. I use all my best spells and defeat them both. I start with a stun, followed by fairy-dust blast, and finally transform them both into weasels. By the end of the lesson I'm almost smiling.

But sometimes I wish I could be as brave in the real world as I am in my games.

When I get home from school Dad's already back from work. I can smell cooking and my nose follows it to the kitchen, like Hansel and Gretel and the breadcrumb trail.

I burst out laughing when I see Dad.

'Why are you wearing a flowery pink-and-green apron?' I ask.

Dad turns to me. 'I don't want to get any sauce on my shirt,' he explains. 'And anyway, what's wrong with my apron?'

'Nothing,' I say with a shrug.

'By the way,' Dad says as I take a seat at the kitchen table, 'what have you done with the cats?'

'What?' I imagine for a moment that all the cats in the world have disappeared, and Dad is blaming me for it.

'Treats . . .' Dad says, which doesn't really explain what he means, but I understand.

'Oh, I . . .' I don't really know how to explain this.

Dad stirs the sauce and pasta, and sits down across from me. 'Is it because of your mum?'

My insides turn to dust. *He must know about the dreams.*

I don't want him to for some reason . . . I like that it's just between Mum and me.

'I don't know what you're talking about,' I say confidently. On TV whenever the police questions anyone, they always deny it. So that's what I plan to do.

'Did I ever tell you the story behind them?'

I frown. Now I'm confused. 'About what?'

'The cats.' Dad sighs, like it's the most obvious thing in the world.

The thing about Dad and me is that we don't talk much, so sometimes our conversations don't go anywhere. If Mum were here right now, she would say something like 'Oh, for goodness' sake, you two, speak in full sentences. Your father is trying to tell you a story,' she would explain to me, rolling her eyes at him. But she would be grinning too, because as much as she moaned at us, she loved us.

'It was the first present your mother ever gave me,' Dad explains. 'She'd decided what we were going to do on our first date.'

Of course, I think. Classic Mum. And suddenly I miss her so much it hurts.

'She wanted us to paint ceramic pots and turned it into a competition. She won, of course. I picked a boring old bowl and painted it plain blue.' Dad's eyes crease as he looks back into a half-remembered past. 'When your mum found a pot with two cats on it, she started jumping up and down excitedly. She always had a way of making even the most normal things fun and magical.'

I watch Dad, spellbound. I'd never really heard any of his stories about Mum before. But I realize now I want to know everything about her. I want to fill my mind with her stories, swim in her past, and fly through the future with her.

'When she finished, I asked her why she picked that pot in particular and she told me that when she was a child there were these two cats that lived near her house. She said they led her to a magical hideaway, where she used to meet with her best friend.' Dad laughs. 'Your mum was always telling stories like that, as if her life was some great big adventure. I never knew which were real and which weren't, but I always enjoyed being a part of them.'

The magic hideaway is real! I want to say. *It is!*

I realize in that moment that I believe it is. And the missing piece slots into place.

These aren't *dreams* I'm having; they're *memories*. And they're of Mum's life when she was my age.

Suddenly I want to watch them all, to know everything I can about Mum. I just need to get through that door.

As Dad carries on cooking my mind drifts back to his story, and I think about how happy they once were.

'Dad?' I say when he starts serving our food.

'Yes?'

'Why did you and Mum split up if you . . . If you loved her so much?'

Dad's face drops, and he turns away. 'It's not that simple, Saff.'

And I can tell from his voice he doesn't want to say any more. But that's OK. Dad has his secrets with Mum, just like I do.

Chapter 16

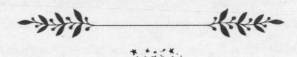

The house is different today, newer. The cracks in the walls have disappeared, and the photos are no longer faded. Like I told Izzy, the doctors gave us good news the other day. Could the house be getting better because Mum is? It is alive after all.

And maybe, just maybe, me playing this game is helping her.

The more I visit, the better Mum seems to be doing.

The tap is running in the bathroom next to the kitchen. I notice it right away, almost like the sound is amplified across the entire house. But I ignore it. Instead I run up, up, up the stairs, all the way to the top of the house. I need to see Mum again, need to try to get to her.

By the time I'm standing in front of her bedroom door I'm out of breath.

The silver branches grow thick up here. I was so

distracted last time that I hadn't noticed. And blooming right above Mum's bedroom door is another yellow flower, just like the one in the courtyard. I seem to notice a new one each time I visit.

The crack on the door is gone, so I can no longer see Mum asleep on her bed. But that's OK, because it's the keyhole I'm looking for. I walk to the door and inspect the golden handle. It has intricately patterned carvings that wind all the way round it.

That's when I realize there's no keyhole. But then, how is it locked?

'Mum?' I call, knocking. 'Mum, open the door!'

Nothing.

I bend down and try to peer through the crack beneath the door. I can see the room, same as before, but from this vantage point I can't get a glimpse of Mum.

I try a few more times to open the door, but it doesn't budge.

Think, Safiya, think.

Could it be magic, like everything else that seems to control the house? Silver branches growing on walls, cats that lead humans to secret hideaways, and swirls of smoke shaped like birds.

I know now this place is magic. And I know it's real. But it's not the sort of magic that comes from wands and spells. It's perfume that holds memories; it's being closer to Mum, and talking to Dad. So then, what is the key to the door?

That's when I feel it, and it's as if the house is answering my question. The damp.

It starts at my toes and works its way up my legs.

I stand up and gasp when I see it. The house is filling up with water. *Fast.*

The stairs below have turned into a pool. The water comes up quickly, threatening to fill the entire house. How is this happening? There are open windows and doors all over. This doesn't make any sense.

The water is slipping through the gap under Mum's bedroom door.

What if it drowns her? The realization lands hard in my chest.

I look down the stairs again. The photos on the walls still hang there, and the furniture below hasn't moved an inch.

The leaves of the silver branches beckon me, like they're asking me to go back down.

Where is all this water coming from? It can't be the tap, can it? It must be . . . but why?

I think back to the bird of smoke, and how it guided me up the stairs to Mum's room. The game was telling me to come here, wasn't it? *Yes.* But then it tried to guide me back down and I . . . ignored it.

Dread surges through me. I made this happen. It's like this really is a game, and I've broken the rules. In *Fairy*

Hunters if you try to cheat, instead of getting kicked out of the game your character is stripped of all but their most basic powers, making it virtually impossible to win.

I was cheating because I was meant to turn the tap off, not come back upstairs. *That's* why the memory faded last time – I wasn't doing the right thing. And now it's trying to warn me again. But what is it trying to tell me?

Think, Safiya, think!

I hit myself on the head, hoping it might knock some sense into me. It does, because I almost poke myself in the eye with the bracelet.

The bracelet! Of course!

When I found the bracelet from the first memory it unlocked the second one.

And when I found the cats from the second memory it unlocked the third.

The aim of the game is to find objects and unlock memories.

And mum's room isn't the *next* level; it's the *boss* level. The final one. *That's* what the bird was trying to show me.

I don't have time to think about it any more, though, as the water is now up to my ankles. I just dive.

The water is cold, but it's a relief from the heat of the day. I try to swim down, but it's harder than it looks, and I float up to the top, splashing around like a duckling.

I try again, this time holding on to the banister. I pull myself down with force, while trying to hold my breath, and use the stairs to guide me down.

I've always been all right at swimming, but I've never had to save someone from drowning. Something takes over my mind, my body, and I push with all my might. I swim down, down, down. Eventually I make it to the bottom of the stairs. Everything looks exactly as it had before the water filled the house. Except it's hazy, like I'm peering through frosted glass.

I look up, and just about see where the water ends towards the top of the house. If I let go of the banister, I'm going to float up, up, up.

I push myself off the bottom of the stairs and try to swim to the bathroom door a few metres away. But, as I kick off the bottom step, my body floats upwards even as I propel myself forward.

I almost make it across. My fingers trace the edges of the door frame, but I can't get a grip, and I float away from it like a discarded piece of rubbish in the ocean.

I'm running out of breath now. I know nothing will happen to me here – it's only a game – but what if something happens to Mum? It's her mind after all. If I run out of breath before I turn off the tap, will it keep running even after I've left the house?

I don't think any more. I don't have time to. I just act.

I let the ceiling of the foyer catch me and kick off it like a frog. My fingers manage to grab the frame of the bathroom door this time. Now I just need to get from there to the tap. I use all my remaining strength to force my body down. I miss the tap the first time and bounce upwards, slamming against the ceiling.

I try again, and this time my fingers clasp it. I'm so happy I could scream with joy, but there isn't enough air left in my lungs. My chest is burning now and I can see spots forming in front of my eyes like stars. I swear I can hear the hospital monitor, like I'm being pulled out of the game.

The tap's slippery, because it's made of metal, but I hook my legs under the sink to keep myself still. I turn, and turn, and turn it off.

The water stops flowing; I can tell because the bubbles have gone. And, just like a giant plug has been released, all the water in the house disappears.

I fall from halfway up the room and collapse on to the floor.

I sit up, gasping for breath, holding on to my throat, but when I look around I'm in the hospital again.

Puddles of water surround Mum's bed. But as soon as I blink they're gone.

I pat myself down and find that I'm entirely dry. Then I check Mum's monitor. I sigh with relief when I see it's all OK. The squiggly line is flowing across the machine steadily, just like before.

She's OK.

Mum's going to be OK.

Chapter 17

'Elle?' I say. 'Elle,' I repeat, but she doesn't answer. I've just spent the last five minutes telling her about Mum's latest hospital news, and all she did was respond with a grunt every few sentences. She hasn't looked up from her phone once, probably because she's busy texting Matty.

'Sorry, Saff,' she says, finally turning her phone face down. 'That's really good!' She grins, pulling me into a hug. At first I'm stiff, but then I soften and hug her back.

We're at mine having our half-term sleepover like we said we would. Elle was the one who brought it up again, which made me happy. I think she still feels kind of bad about the perfume thing, so she's trying to make it up to me. But it feels different to usual. Even though Matty's not physically here it's like he's taken over the entire evening. Either Elle's texting him, or I'm thinking about ways to bring up the mean things he said. I want to show Elle what sort of person he really is, but whenever I try to speak it's like my lips are glued shut.

With Mum at the hospital, and my friendship group falling apart, it feels like my world is crumbling like the ruined fairy palace – like the only thing in my life that makes sense is the house with the memories and the game.

But the doctors said that Mum's doing as well as she can. They use words like 'stable' and 'progress'. I need to focus on my mission: watch the memories and collect the objects. I can't let myself get distracted again. Not by the door, or anything else. Because I'm certain that, once I get through all the memories, the door will open. And when the door opens . . .

'You can pick the film tonight!' Elle says, crashing into my thoughts like ocean waves against a rock. 'Matt's gone to the cinema to watch a double screening of *Star Wars*. He's so lame – he *actually* turns his phone off for it. Shall we get into our PJs?'

Finally. Finally we can start our sleepover properly. Even though it's only because Elle's boyfriend won't be in virtual contact for five hours.

'Yeah!' I say excitedly, jumping up and down. 'Shall we have cheese and Marmite toasties?' I ask a little tentatively, worried she won't remember that it was always our favourite snack.

Elle's eyes light up like she's eleven again. 'I forgot about those! Please can we?'

Ten minutes later we're in our PJs and in the kitchen armed with butter and bread, ready to make our toasties.

'Where's the Marmite?' Elle asks, sifting through the cupboards, glancing over at me through her nerd glasses. They really suit her, but she never wears them out. I'm pretty sure most people in our year don't even realize she needs them. I wear mine all the time.

'In the fridge.'

Elle wrinkles her nose. 'Weirdo.'

I laugh.

Lady waltzes up to Elle shyly, wagging her tail and fluttering her little eyelashes. She's such a charmer.

'Hello, beautiful!' Elle says, bending down to stroke her. She talks in this funny voice she reserves only for Lady. It's silly and cute. I can't help but think how different Elle is on any given day. How she moulds to whoever she's around.

Here, though, it feels like this is the real Elle: glasses, mismatched PJs and all. But for some reason she can't let anyone else see the real her.

The Elle who has an irrational fear of tiny holes (she literally can't eat holey cheese). Trypophobia, it's called.

The Elle who sometimes talks in her sleep.

The Elle who secretly wishes her dad cared a bit less about work.

'So,' she says when she's finished fussing Lady and has

retrieved the Marmite from the fridge. 'What film shall we watch?'

'*Spirited Away?*' I ask hopefully.

Elle rolls her eyes. 'Again, Saff? We've seen it a hundred times. And anyway, we're too old for cartoons now.'

Cartoons. Elle clearly doesn't appreciate the skill that goes into animated films. Especially Studio Ghibli films, which are essentially masterpieces.

I shrug. 'You decide then,' I say, trying to keep my voice even. She said I could pick but I know she'll just disagree with all my choices.

I can't help but feel like the mood's turned again, like a storm cloud has emerged in the kitchen.

Elle eventually chooses for us. An action film Matty recommended. We watch it in bed with our toasties and I try to make out like it's one of our old sleepovers, but it isn't. There's no funny commentary from Elle, no feet fights under the blanket. We just sit there silently and watch the film. Who actually does that?

And, even though she knows Matty's phone is off, Elle still checks hers every few minutes.

I've started to question recently whether Elle and I would even be friends if we met now and not at primary school. Sometimes it feels as if I'm trying to put together broken pieces of our old friendship, but they no longer fit.

Izzy messages me just then.

Izzy: SAFF. Why didn't you tell me how good Princess Mononoke *is? I'm in tears!!!*

I grin. She sends me a photo of her crying, her pet guinea pig cuddled up on her lap.

Saff: My Neighbor Totoro is still my favourite. How many have you watched now? Five?!?!
Izzy: Six. How's your mum? And having fun at your sleepover?

I avoid answering her second question. Instead I give her a quick update on Mum and tell her about the film we're watching.

Izzy: Sounds . . . interesting.

She streams it too and we send each other funny messages about how awful it is, just like I used to do with Elle.

Later on I suggest a game as Elle and I wait to fall asleep.

'Would you rather eat poo-flavoured chocolate or chocolate-flavoured poo?' I ask her.

'What?' Elle says.

I explain the rules. You have to give two different options that are equally as bad, and see which one the other person picks.

Elle laughs. 'That sounds silly,' she says dismissively,

reminding me of Abir.

'I would have chocolate-flavoured poo,' I say, ignoring her judgement. But my cheeks are burning and I feel stupid now.

'Fair enough.' Elle yawns, signalling the end of the game.

It's after a few moments of silence that I finally feel brave enough to say something about Matty.

'Elle?' I turn to my side, facing her.

She's laid flat, looking up at the ceiling. 'Yeah?'

I sigh.

'What is it?' she hisses, and I can't tell whether she's irritated at me, or worried about what I have to say. For the first time in forever I'm not sure she's enjoying our sleepover at all, and it makes my stomach squirm.

'I . . .' *Don't chicken out, Saff. Don't chicken out.* 'I was in ICT. I was sitting next to Matty and David and I saw something on Matty's phone.'

I can feel Elle bristle next to me.

'What?' Her voice is sharp, like a knife, but for some reason I feel like it's pointed at me.

I tell her about the photo and how they were laughing at it. And I tell her what Matty said to me, and about Jonnie's joke at the bike shed.

'Oh my gosh, Saff,' Elle says, and I expect her to reassure me that it was horrible, and that she's going to talk to Matty about it. The old Elle would. But she doesn't. 'I got worried you were going to say something bad, like he was texting some other girl!' She takes a relieved breath, and then carries on. 'Don't worry. Matty and Jonnie are like it with everyone,' Elle assures me. 'The other day they were making fun of me for being ginger and pale . . . It's just what they're like.'

She looks at me expectantly, so I say the first thing that's on my mind. 'But that's not . . . very nice, is it?'

'Come on, Saff.' Elle pouts. 'Don't be so boring!' She reaches out for me, but I pull away. That's when I see her roll her eyes. 'Wow. OK. You know what? Ever since I started going out with Matty all you've done is moan. You never ask me about him, or how things are going . . . You're just jealous that I have a boyfriend and you don't.'

'Why did you tell Abir and not me?' I blurt.

'What?' Elle looks genuinely confused, so I explain how I saw them both whispering the day we walked to the bike shed.

Elle shrugs. 'I suppose I thought she would understand a bit more. I was right.'

My heart pounds with every word of Elle's. I feel sick, kind of like when you eat too many sweets. Maybe she's right. Maybe I have been too negative about everything, thinking about us and our friendship instead of her. I feel guilty about being such a bad friend. After all, everyone else seems happy for her and Matty. Everyone but me.

'Elle –'

'Whatever,' Elle mutters, purposefully turning away from me. 'I'm tired anyway.'

'I'm sor–'

'Goodnight!' Her voice rings across my room, bouncing off the walls in its false cheeriness. Then it floats down and settles on to us like a bitter smell I can't quite get rid of.

I know not to push this with Elle. Not now. So I don't.

Instead I turn the other way and think about Mum again, and how she's trapped in that room alone. It's like she's some sort of fairy-tale princess. Like Rapunzel.

That's when it hits me. Mum's kind of like Sleeping Beauty in her tower, waiting for her prince to come and rescue her.

What if I'm the prince?

I realize now that I know how to win the game. I need to watch all the memories and unlock the door. And when the door opens . . . I'm going to save Mum. I'm going to wake her up.

But not just in the game, in the *real* world too.

Chapter 18

When I wake up the next morning Elle's already gone.

I check my phone to see if she sent me any messages, but she hasn't, so I decide to give her some space. I spend far too long thinking about what I said to her, trying to figure out where I went wrong. Did I sound bitter about Matty? Should I have asked more about the film he went to watch at the cinema?

I have a few hours before I'm supposed to go to the hospital to visit Mum, so I decide to distract myself by playing *Fairy Hunters*. It works. The familiar landscape takes over my bedroom and I'm transported, again, to another world. I cast spells and block them too; I protect my nest from rogue wizards and get most valuable player three times; I rank up a level, which means I have access to even better spells and protective gear. It's just as I'm finally starting to feel better about Elle that I get a weird message from Izzy.

Izzy: Sorry you couldn't come today! I was looking forward to seeing you . . . xx

That's when I see it. Elle's been uploading photos all afternoon of her, Abir and Izzy. Pictures of them at a coffee shop, Elle with her arms around Abir. Pictures of them walking down our local high street, arms linked.

Why did they go without me? And why did Elle tell Izzy I couldn't go?

Because she didn't want you there, a voice in my head tells me.

The realization feels like a woodpecker is chipping away at my heart, but I keep looking anyway. There's a photo of Elle in a changing room, posing in front of the mirror. She runs a poll: *Should I buy this dress?* I vote yes, hoping she'll notice me. Maybe then she'll ask me to come to town and meet them. Maybe she'll say she meant to invite me after all, and it was all a mistake.

My broken heart sinks down to my stomach when I see the last photo. Matty and Jonnie have joined them now. Is she going to tell them about what I said? Are they all going to laugh at me? I feel sick.

I try to calm myself down. Elle's my best friend, she wouldn't do that. Would she?

*

When I get to the hospital a couple of hours later the reception desk is empty, so I wait on a chair across from it and check my phone. Elle hasn't uploaded any more photos.

I glance at the old man, the one I saw on the very first day. He's sleeping. A pile of fresh books have been laid out for him. To pass the time I try to read the titles from where I'm sitting.

After a few minutes no one turns up and I'm starting to feel impatient. I stand up and look around to find someone – anyone – to help me, before returning to my seat. Eventually a doctor walks out, swinging the doors wide open. He's in a rush and as soon as he walks past me I bolt for them, grabbing the handle just in time to stop the censor shutting me out again.

I walk down the long hall, half jogging. Then I turn the corner and into Mum's room, my feet skidding across the floor from the momentum. Her curtains are pulled across, which is strange. Usually that means someone's visiting.

For a moment I'm worried someone's here. I need to be alone. But when I pull them back her bed is empty.

'What?' I yell so loudly that a nurse from the other room walks in. It's Edward. I'm relieved to see his familiar face, but my panic is growing like the tallest tree. Has something happened to her?

'Where's my mum? She hasn't . . . She's not . . .' I let the words fade away.

Is this because of the water? Did Mum drown in the dream? Was I too late? If something's happened to her now I'll *know* it's all my fault, because Mum was getting better!

Chapter 19

'**G**oodness no!' Edward walks over to me. 'Is that what you . . . ?' He looks like he wants to pull me in for a hug. 'You poor thing! Why didn't they tell you at reception?'

I shrug, hoping he won't pry. I don't want him to know I snuck in. 'Tell me what?' I ask instead.

Edward smiles and it eases my mind a little. 'They've moved your mum to a different ward. She's on the other side of the hospital now.'

Is that good or bad?

'It's a good thing,' Edward says, as if reading my mind. He goes on to explain that they've reduced Mum's medicine and the levels of support she's getting from the ventilator, which is the machine that helps her breathe. Apparently they're going to put something called a tracheostomy in to replace it. 'I can take you there now. I was just finishing my shift anyway.'

I smile, relieved. 'Thank you.'

We don't talk as we walk back down the hall, the echo of our footsteps breaking the silence. For a moment I really thought she'd . . . that she had . . . I brush the thought aside.

We walk to the other end of the hospital and go through a final set of doors into a different ward. It looks shinier, newer.

Edward lets me in, then says a quick goodbye. He shuts the door after him and, for the first time since seeing Mum in the hospital, we have complete privacy. There is only one other bed in here and it isn't occupied right now.

The walls here are lilac, much better than the custard ones everywhere else. I walk over to the window and watch the setting sun. The view is nicer here too. Instead of the concrete car park, this part of the hospital overlooks a green field, cows grazing in the distance.

I look back at Mum. I want her to open her eyes and see it. I want her to watch the sunset with me.

There's a chair next to Mum's bed and I settle into it.

I lean into my pocket and pull out . . . the perfume. It's not here. The cushion and blanket I brought on the second visit are, but not the perfume.

I check my backpack, but nothing's there. My stomach drops. *Where is it?*

That's when I remember that I left it in the bedside drawer in Mum's old ward during my last visit. I check the drawers in here. It's not in either of them. I check under the bed and in the little cupboard of spare pillows. I check every part of the room until I'm definitely sure it's not in here.

I can't visit Aminah without the perfume; I can't watch the next memory and unlock her bedroom door. What if Mum really is improving because I've been playing the game? And what if this makes all the good that's happening turn bad?

Without the memories I can't wake her up.

No, no, no! my brain cries out, but outwardly I try to stay calm.

I can see the reception desk through the narrow glass pane of the hospital door. It sits right across from Mum's room. There's a nurse I don't recognize. I can see the top of her hair, her curly fringe bouncing as she bobs her head.

I run out to her. 'Excuse me?' I say.

She holds her hand up to silence me. That's when I notice she's on the phone.

I wait, tapping my foot, panic taking over as I hear her speak.

'Yes, you can find a list of visiting hours on our website. Is there anything else I can do for you?' Her voice is all friendly and inviting. 'Yes, of course I can give you a care summary now. Bear with me please, sir.'

She tap, tap, taps on her computer for a moment, all the while pretending I'm not standing there. 'Thank you for waiting,' she says in a sing-song voice to whoever is on the phone. The nurse spends another minute talking, and I don't really know what to do with myself – so I just stand, arms crossed, back against the wall.

Eventually she puts the phone down and I go to address her, but she stands up and leaves the reception area to go into a room across the hall. I watch her lazy steps as if she has all the time in the world.

I can feel the monster crawl up through my ribcage, the way it does when my blood starts to boil. I swallow it down, along with the panic, and it slides back into the pit of my stomach. I can almost feel the thud as it lands, making me nauseated.

The nurse sits back down again, but instead of speaking to me she resumes typing. Then she folds her arms and looks up at me. 'Can I help?' she finally asks.

'My mum's in that room,' I explain, pointing behind me. 'She was just moved over, I think. But there's something important that's gone missing –'

'If you would like to file a complaint, you'll have to go online and –'

I frown at her. 'It's not that,' I snap, clenching my teeth together to bite the irritation down. 'I left it in the drawer in her old room. I just wondered whether there was any way to go and get it?'

'Well, I'm afraid you can't go into a ward unless you're a visitor,' she says.

I wait for her to continue, to offer a solution, but she doesn't.

'I know that,' I say slowly, trying to keep calm. 'I just wondered when we would be able to get it back?'

'I'll have to check with one of the nurses,' she says, turning back to her computer.

I wait. She doesn't say anything else.

'Did you want to know what ward it was on?' I ask.

'That would be an idea.' The woman smiles, but it's not very kind. I notice the name on her badge: Sue.

I tell her and a couple of minutes later, after she makes a quick call, Sue says, 'One of the nurses is going to have a look and bring it over when they can.'

'Thank you,' I say, even as my insides are screaming.

So, all I can to do now is wait.

Back in the room I sit back down next to Mum. I look at her, realizing I haven't done that in a while; I've been too preoccupied with Aminah.

'Hi, Mum,' I begin. My voice is a little hoarse. For some reason there are tears in my eyes almost immediately, like they'd been waiting for the right moment to fall. 'Mum, I'm sorry.'

I think of all the things I have to be sorry for, and it drags up emotions I had buried, like seashells at the bottom of the ocean. For not visiting her that day or sending her a message. For not taking the time to talk to her, hug her. For making her feel jealous of Dad. For treating our weekly visits like a chore. Finally I know what it is I need to say. It's simple. 'I'm sorry I've pushed you away all these years.'

I think back to all those moments I could have got to know her more. I was so used to her being around, so used to her asking questions and pushing things with us, that I forgot to push back.

Then I think about the argument and the final words I said to Mum before she went into hospital. I know I need to face it. And today, without the memories to hide behind, I'm ready.

'I love Dad more than I love you! I understand him and he understands me. We –' I waved my arms between us – 'we're too different. You come from a different world.'

Each time I spoke must've been like a punch in the gut.

Mum was crying. 'You're right,' she said. 'I do. I had a whole life before you, Safiya. Everything you're doing now, feeling now, I've done it and felt it too.'

Her voice was shaking, but I pushed and pushed and pushed.

I told her I didn't care what she had to say, and I was fed up of visiting her every weekend. And she just stood there and listened.

'We're more alike than you think,' Mum said when I eventually stopped. She wiped her tears away with her sleeve. 'And no matter what you say about any of that I love you.'

I should've said it back. I should've said 'I love you.'

But I didn't. Instead I left.

'I love you,' I say now, hoping it's not too late.

Amanda comes in soon after and I stand up. She's holding the perfume in both of her palms like it's the most precious thing in the world.

'Safiya!' she says, seemingly pleased to see me. 'When I heard whose bed it was I wanted to fetch it myself.' Amanda's voice always goes up at the end of her sentences, so it's kind of like we're in a Disney film and she's singing about our day. 'You're doing great,' she adds, handing me the bottle. I almost expect a bunch of woodland creatures to jump on to her shoulders, lift it from her hands and transport it to mine. 'Collecting all your mum's things for her, bringing them here for her. It all helps with the recovery. Keep going!'

Amanda leaves soon after, but her words linger in my mind.

I can make this up to Mum, and I will.

I use one drop of perfume on her forehead. I wipe it across with my fingers, caressing her face.

I lean down and give her a kiss on her brow.

And almost immediately I drift, drift, drift . . .

Chapter 20

The house is back to normal now, and it's as if it had never started falling apart, or flooded right up to the ceiling. Everything was OK in the end. Still, I'm mad at myself for wasting time on the door when I could have been collecting memories and objects.

There's no more time to waste. I run across the foyer to the bathroom, where the tap is flowing again. Already the sink is full, spilling on to the bathroom floor.

I step over the puddles and turn the tap off. The change is small, but I can feel it, almost as if it's a part of me. The steady heartbeat of the house picks up pace, like the crescendo in a happy song. And I feel ready, ready for what's to come.

'What are you doing?' Zaina asks Aminah, who is trying her best to tame her hair in the bathroom mirror.

'Nothing,' Aminah responds, not even glancing at her.

'Where are you going?' Zaina hops around her sister, questions tumbling out of her mouth.

'Nowhere.'

Zaina pouts. 'Can I come?'

'No.'

'Why?'

'Because I'm not going anywhere!' Aminah's annoyed now. She finishes at the mirror, and turns to Zaina, frowning.

She's silent for a moment, and then rearranges her face into a smile. 'Tell you what,' she says, her voice rising an octave. 'Why don't you braid my hair for me?'

Zaina's face lights up. 'Really?' she asks, as if the suggestion is too good to be true.

Aminah nods, her smile shark-like.

I narrow my eyes. Something seems . . . off.

As soon as Zaina skips up the stairs to get a brush and some hair bobbles, Aminah bolts out of the bathroom and rushes to the courtyard outside. She's already scaled the wall before I make it out after her.

'Sorry I'm late,' Aminah tells Rawan once she's settled under the canopy of leaves. 'My sister was being annoying. I had to get rid of her. If she found out about this place, she would never leave us alone.'

'It's OK,' Rawan says. She's silent for just a beat too long. 'I kind of have a surprise for you . . .'

Aminah raises her eyebrows. 'You're finally going to assassinate me?' she jokes.

Rawan laughs, and I can see how comfortable the two are around one another. I wonder how much time has passed since the last memory.

Rawan answers the question for me, like she heard my thoughts.

'How long have we been friends now?' she asks.

Aminah shrugs. 'Few weeks?'

Rawan nods. 'Well, I've been keeping a bit of a secret from you this whole time,' she admits.

'You're a ghost?'

Rawan shakes her head.

'You're actually an alien in human skin?'

'Closer,' Rawan says. 'But not quite.'

Aminah looks a little nervous now. 'What is it?' she asks, frowning, her humour gone.

'I'm in a theatre group!' Rawan declares, handing Aminah a flyer.

I peer over at it.

THE SECRET THEATRE PRESENTS
RAPUNZEL
27 AUGUST 7.30 P.M.
LOCATION
?

Aminah laughs, looking relieved. 'This is . . . not what I expected you to say.'

Rawan raises her eyebrows. 'What did you think I would say?'

Aminah shrugs. 'That you were moving away or something. Anyway,' she continues, 'why is there a question mark next to the location?'

'Well . . . it's a secret theatre, so you keep the location hidden.'

'Why is it a secret?'

Rawan shrugs this time. 'Because that makes it more magical.'

'Rawan,' Aminah says, after inspecting the flyer, 'this is impressive.'

Rawan beams at her. 'There are two other girls who are doing it with me, Hana and Ib, and they're really cool.'

'You have *other* friends?' Aminah puts her hand to her heart, her expression scandalized. 'How dare you!'

Rawan laughs.

'So, when can I watch the play?'

'Well . . .' Rawan takes a deep breath. 'Tonight, actually, if you like. When we rehearse.'

Aminah looks serious for a moment. 'I'll have to get away from my sister somehow – she's so nosy – but that should be fine!'

'There's more . . .' Rawan says, twisting her fingers round the bottom of her top. 'Would you . . . would you want to play the main character, Rapunzel?' Aminah's jaw drops. 'Someone dropped out last minute . . . We're kind of desperate.'

Aminah frowns.

'I'm the prince,' Rawan explains in a rush. 'So you'll mainly be acting with me. Pretty please?'

'Why can't one of the others do it? I've never acted before!'

Rawan sighs. 'They don't want to. Come on, it'll be fun!'

Aminah is thoughtful for some time. 'I'll try . . . but I can't promise anything.'

'Great!' Rawan says, overjoyed. 'Perfect.'

'On one condition,' Aminah adds, smirking.

'Anything,' Rawan answers solemnly.

'*You* bring the snacks next time.'

Rawan and Aminah fall into a contemplative silence as Aminah presents her with flasks of saffron tea and sugar sweets stolen from the kitchen.

'This could be good actually . . .' Aminah says, sipping her drink. 'I need an extracurricular anyway, to apply to schools in England.'

But the words are barely out of her mouth before a great big crash sounds just over the wall by Aminah's house.

I jump, sand flying everywhere.

'What was that?' Rawan frowns.

Aminah runs up to the wall and pulls herself up, peering

over it. The slide has toppled to the ground. I glance across the courtyard and see something move out of the corner of my eye, right by the kitchen door. But it's too fast and by the time I turn to look, it's gone.

'It was just the cats,' Aminah answers, relief evident in her voice.

I follow her eyes. The two cats are sniffing round the slide, looking very guilty.

Aminah and I take our seats back across from Rawan.

The memory starts to fade as the pair discuss their first group rehearsal that very night.

'Where are we holding it?' Aminah asks. 'I almost forgot to ask!'

'Here, at midnight. When everyone else is asleep.'

Aminah laughs. 'OK, Cinderella. Midnight it is.'

Chapter 21

As I walk into Mum's flat I swear I can see the silver branches along her walls, the yellow flowers that sprout anew each time I unlock another memory. I can see a mound of sand where her coffee table usually stands; palm trees hang down instead of her lamp and television. And at the very centre of the room are Rawan and Aminah, exactly as they were in the last memory.

But then I blink and they're gone. The living room is back to normal.

I think back to the house, and the memories, and try to figure out what I need to do next. I thought I was supposed to collect the objects that unlocked the memories. The bracelet and the cat kind of worked in that way. But the third memory was unlocked by a tap. And I can't exactly collect the tap from Mum's old house, can I?

That's how I know I've been looking at it wrong. It's not about the objects that unlock the memories; it's about what's *in* the memories. That's how cutscenes in games work. They give you clues, but you need to watch the cutscenes carefully to know what your mission is about.

In the first memory Zaina stole Aminah's bracelet and that's why they were arguing.

In the second memory Rawan challenged Aminah to pet one of the cats, and that's how they became friends.

So what happened in the third memory? Rawan asked Aminah to join the play. But what object could be linked to it? What do I need to find to unlock the next memory?

I know the right answer will come to me, but I don't have it just yet, so I decide to search Mum's flat in the hope that something will jump out at me.

I start at the front door and work my way through Mum's flat methodically. I look in every drawer searching for *something*. Except I don't know what that is just yet. I move from the living room to the kitchen and back again. I try fridge magnets, cutlery, the medicine box, old magazines. I even look in all the plant pots and under the sofa.

Next I try Mum's bedroom. I start in her wardrobe, hoping to find some old box with trinkets in it. Secret items Mum didn't want anyone else to see. It feels wrong, like I'm invading her privacy, but I keep telling myself that I'm doing this to save her. And there's this other part of me that wants to find out more, like the memories have woken up something inside me.

The wardrobe door isn't fully shut and when I pull it open Mum's clothes spill out, a pile crumpled at the bottom where they've fallen off the hanger. I start rummaging at the back and get excited when my hands grasp something solid. *Yes.* I pull it out to find it's a shoebox. The perfect place to hide your secrets. But when I open it, to my disappointment, I find a pair of shoes.

I change tack, removing everything from Mum's wardrobe, even patting down the wood for a secret compartment. I feel bad about making a mess, so I spend double the time hanging everything back up, until it looks better than how Mum left it.

I spot a beautiful green-and-blue beaded mermaid-style dress Mum has from Kuwait. It's glittery and shiny and looks like scales covered in gold and gems. I remember Mum wearing it years ago when I was very little, but I had forgotten about it.

After a moment I reluctantly shut the wardrobe door and keep searching. My arms ache now and I've found nothing.

I move over to Mum's chest of drawers. Then I try under the bed, on top of the wardrobe, in the bathroom cupboards. I check all her folders and photos lying round the house. I even check the toilet cistern before I realize how ridiculous this has become. I'm a little manic, like a detective searching for clues.

I stomp around the flat like an angry bear, until I collapse on the sofa in a heap. *Think, Safiya, think.*

I look across at Mum's bookshelves and spot a photo album sitting next to an old copy of *The Wizard of Oz*. I rush over and look through the album carefully, but none of photos are from when Mum was my age. It's like there's a great big black hole swallowing up that part of her past. There are photos of Mum as a toddler, but then they skip to Mum at university, and Mum after she met Dad.

Why would she keep these if she's not with Dad any more . . . ? I think back to the way Dad spoke about Mum, and how he said it was complicated. Maybe she does still love him? Maybe things aren't as simple as I thought . . .

Just then I get a message from Elle.

My heart practically leaps from my chest. I haven't heard from her since our sleepover, and that went so badly I'm scared to read what she has to say.

Elle: Hey, Saff. Miss you this week. <3 Me and the girls were talking and we thought it would be cool to end half-term by going to Maccies and then the cinema with some of the boys? Matty's going to be there, of course. It might be a good time for you two to make up?

I frown, a little confused by almost everything she's said. First of all, when has she been chatting to the girls without me?

Secondly, 'Matty's going to be there, of course'. I'm the one who's been her best friend for over half our lives. Not *him*.

And what does she mean by make up? I never realized we'd fallen out . . . Has she told him about what I said?

I reply to Elle's message all nice and sweet, but inside I'm burning. The truth is, I'm scared about what's going to happen between me and Elle if I don't go. And I need to figure things out with her, even if it means being around Matty.

Safiya: Miss you too <3. Sounds great! When are we going? X

Elle sends back a virtual invitation to the event, like it's a birthday party and not some sort of casual hang-out. That's when it hits me.

The flyer for the play. *That* must be the object linked to the last memory.

I shove my phone aside and grab Mum's laptop. It's still on her coffee table from before she went to the hospital. It's dead, so I look for the charger. Mum's so messy and random that I end up finding it in the cupboard with her mugs after about ten minutes of searching.

I pace up and down her living room while I wait for the laptop to get enough charge to turn on. When it does I'm relieved to see she hasn't set a password. I manage to get on it without any trouble. I cross my fingers and hope to find the person I'm looking for . . .

I look for her name in Mum's emails and a whole stream of messages come up.

The most recent one is dated just a month ago. They've kept in contact for all these years. *That's* true friendship.

I don't read Mum's emails, because that feels too personal, but I copy Rawan's email address and start drafting a message from my phone.

Hi Rawan,
You might know who I am . . .

Chapter 22

'Are you sure you want to get all of that?' Elle whispers from behind me. We're at Maccies with the others and I'm just about to buy a burger and chips.

'I thought we came here to eat?' I retort.

Our Maccies is always busy. Tonight it's full of people our age, though I don't recognize most of them. They must go to a different school.

'Yeah, but I'm just getting chips. I don't want to look greedy,' Elle says.

I roll my eyes (when she's not looking). I realize, in that moment, that our Friday-night sleepovers are well and truly over.

'Well, I haven't eaten since lunch, so I'm buying a burger.'

Before all of this, everything with Mum, a comment like

that from Elle would make me second-guess my decision. Today it doesn't.

Elle shrugs, already back on her phone. Matty isn't here yet, so I know exactly who she's texting. It doesn't bother me today, though, because I'm checking my phone too. I emailed Rawan asking her if she had a copy of the flyer she and Mum used for the play.

I didn't say *exactly* why I needed it, only that it was going in a memory box I was making for Mum. It's kind of true, I guess. I'm turning the old hat box I put the ceramic cats in into a memory box, seeing as everything in it is from Mum's memories.

I've been calling it my inventory, like in *Fairy Hunters*, where you collect spells and food and clothes to help you on your mission. Sometimes you get crystals too, and rare items.

My inventory holds the perfume bottle, the bracelet and the cats, and soon it'll hold the flyer too. When I'm done collecting all of the objects I'm going to take the box to the hospital to show Mum, and that's when the door will open!

Rawan was upset to hear that Mum is ill, especially as she's in Kuwait and can't see her, but I told her she's getting better. It's been exactly three days since Rawan sent the flyer. She's tracking the delivery and told me she'd let me know once it arrived. This morning the flyer was somewhere in London, so it's probably on its way here. I've been checking my phone obsessively all day, waiting for updates. I can't bear another day without a new memory.

As Elle and I take our seats, and I start eating, the boys arrive. My heart sinks as I see Jonnie among them. At least David's here, though. I still remember him asking about Mum. Maybe he won't be as mean.

Matty kisses Elle right on the lips in front of everyone, looking around afterwards to make sure we saw.

Izzy's sitting right across from me and we exchange a look. She smirks, and I know exactly what she's thinking.

The boys come back with their food. They haven't ordered much either. So now I'm just sat here, scoffing my burger, while the rest of them pick at a bag of chips like pigeons.

'Just like you to be hungry, Dobby,' Jonnie says, smiling. But it's not friendly. He's teeth are jagged at the end, like some sort of predator.

Abir laughs, Izzy frowns, Elle ignores the comment. She's too busy staring lovingly into Matty's eyes while they feed each other chips. I want to believe that she didn't hear it, but I'm not so sure any more.

'Hilarious,' I say sarcastically.

Jonnie laughs. 'Someone's a bit *sensitive*, aren't they?'

I shrug, looking him dead in the eye. 'No, I just don't think you're funny.'

Abir lets out a sigh. 'Just ignore him,' she hisses at me.

'Jonnie's an idiot to everyone.'

'Abir finds me funny, don't you?' Jonnie presses, noticing the tension between us.

David shrinks back into his seat, looking miserable. He opens his mouth as if to say something, but then takes a sip of his drink instead.

'Abir would find a plastic bag funny,' I retort, before I have the chance to think. The monster swims triumphantly through my veins, egging me on.

She gasps as if I've slapped her.

I open my mouth to say something more, but everyone's turned to stare at someone who just walked in.

I look. It's Charlotte, the girl Matty was making fun of in our ICT lesson. She's with another girl in our year, Gini, queuing up for food. Actual food, it seems, not just chips.

'All right, Charlotte?' Jonnie says, ever the one to start trouble.

Charlotte turns and sees the group. Her shoulders droop, and she pulls her hair in front of her face, like maybe she knows about the horrible things the boys have been saying about her.

I see us from her eyes. Intimidating. Mean.

I watch Matty nudge Jonnie and point to Charlotte. He puts his phone down, just as she picks hers up.

It can't be a coincidence, can it?

I watch her read something on it. Her face crumples, and I know it's bad.

She shows Gini, who glances over at us, annoyed, but she's probably too scared to do anything about it. They don't end up getting any food. Instead they just leave. I watch them go, my eyes travelling across the room, and that's when I see her.

Aminah, sitting in a booth alone.

The way the light falls on her it's like she's glowing, like one of the fire fairies from *Fairy Hunters*. Someone crosses my path and I lose sight of her for a second. When I look back at the booth she's gone.

But she gives me all the courage I need.

Without thinking I snatch Matty's phone from where it sits in front of him, and read the message he sent to Charlotte aloud. After I'm done, and everyone falls silent, I show them the photo he took in ICT, embellishments and all.

Then I go through the others one by one. It's not that difficult to find because Matty's saved them all in a special folder.

Everyone's so shocked that no one even tries to snatch the phone off me. They just listen.

Finally I find the photo of me. They've photoshopped my eyes so they're bigger than normal and green, instead of brown. They've removed my hair so it looks like I'm bald and written a silly caption under it.

I realize now I wasn't being a bad friend at all. I wasn't jealous about Matty, I was just being honest.

When I'm done I turn to Elle. 'So?' I say. My whole body feels like it's made of electricity. 'Do you still want to be his girlfriend after that?'

Elle goes beetroot red as everyone turns to look at her. She pauses for what seems like a million years, and then finally answers. 'Don't be so dramatic, Saff,' she says, her voice cold. 'It's just a laugh.'

'I'm not being dramatic.' I snap, my voice ringing loud and clear. 'You're just being fake, and mean. Where's the Elle that always makes up stupid puns? Where's the Elle that sings songs with me in silly voices, or the one who didn't care so much what everyone thought of her?' While I'm talking Elle's eyes flit left and right, and she goes redder and redder. She looks at me for a moment like she misses all that too, but then she glances at Abir and Matty, and says nothing.

I slide out of the booth without another word. Elle doesn't even try to stop me.

As I reach the door I glance back at her. She catches my eye for a moment before turning to Matty again. It's as if I was never there at all; the gap I left has already been filled.

Dad picks me up soon after and we go home. I head straight to my room, Lady bounding in after me.

I'm about to disappear into a game, to try to forget the world, but there's a package on my bed. My hands shake as I pick it up. I pull out the flyer and find that it's exactly as it appeared in the memory.

THE SECRET THEATRE PRESENTS

RAPUNZEL

27 AUGUST 7.30 P.M.

LOCATION

?

And, even though today's been the worst, it's been the best too. Not only can I unlock the next memory, but I finally know what it's all leading to: a play! A play Mum performed with her friends.

Chapter 23

'I'm Hana,' a confident girl in a glittery red headscarf announces, shaking Aminah's hand formally. I can't help but giggle as she kisses her on both cheeks, like they're grown-ups, even though she looks about our age. Her Arabic is much more pronounced than the others, whose accents have a slight American lilt to them.

The other girl, Ibtisam, introduces herself next, much more casually than her friend. 'But you can call me Ib,' she says, grinning at Aminah.

Hana waves a hand dismissively. 'I prefer Ibtisam. It has more to it, don't you think?'

'I . . . guess so,' Aminah agrees, her eyes darting between the two, clearly unsure which one to appease.

Ib laughs. 'Thanks, Hana, for telling me how to pronounce my own name.' She rolls her eyes, though her voice is affectionate.

Once the introductions are done, Rawan clears her throat. 'So, are we ready for our first rehearsal?'

All three girls nod in unison.

'I should start by explaining to Aminah why we picked *Rapunzel*,' Rawan says.

'Because Hana makes a really good witch,' Ib grins, turning to Aminah. 'You'll see.'

Hana glares at her, then turns to Aminah too. 'She's right, I do! So don't cross me.'

'But also,' Rawan interjects, 'I think fairy tales are just magical. And they teach us about life. Rapunzel has to fend for herself, and she realizes there's so much more to the world than she first imagined.'

Everyone falls silent for a moment, and the only sound is an orchestra of grasshoppers playing into the night.

But then Hana waves her hands, like a bossy wizard casting a spell. 'Right. Let's begin!'

The moon and stars shine bright and the air is warm as Aminah, Rawan and the others rehearse their scenes. Each of them holds a flashlight that they shine on their scripts while they recite their lines.

As the girls act out the scenes something spectacular happens. The silver branches, in bloom with dozens of yellow flowers now, slither down from the wall and on to the sand. The branches rise up, circling around the troupe, until they resemble a tall tower in the middle of a forest clearing – like a theatre set made entirely of wood.

I know this is all part of Mum's imagination, filling in the gaps with wonder and magic.

Hana enters the set as the witch, and Rawan helps Aminah through her lines before taking up her role as the prince. From her bag she pulls a very real string of beautifully patterned materials all tied together, which Aminah plaits into her hair. She throws it down for Rawan to climb.

The branches transition seamlessly every time the scene changes – their silver light shines down on the girls making them glow, though this part of the play exists only for my eyes. This world in Mum's mind is filled with her memories, but they're different.

When I think back to some of the best and worst moments of my life I don't really imagine them how they happened. I imagine them a bit different, more magical. Like the time I went to a birthday party at the local swimming pool. We were all mermaids chased by a deadly shark, then we were pirates searching for lost treasure.

Mum's memories are a little like that, and this one is the most magical one I've experienced so far. Like it's extra special.

Then comes a scene where the witch finds out Rapunzel has been meeting with the prince. In this version she tells her she will never ever leave, because she's going to lock her up and throw away the key.

And I can't help but think about Mum at the top of the house, trapped behind her bedroom door. All I want to do is unlock it and free her. All I want is for her to wake up.

The branches shine silver still, but an inky black courses through them like veins, and they look entirely alive. I reach out and they feel like the slimy skin of a frog. The witch pulls Mum to the darkest corner, and drags her into a room in the great big tower.

The memory makes it look all too real, though, and I run to the witch.

'Stop it!' I call, trying to pull her away from Mum.

The witch does what I say, like she's heard me. She turns, facing me, and for one moment my heart freezes.

But then she looks upwards, beyond the wall, frowning. 'What was that?' she says, and she's no longer the witch any more, and they're no longer in the tower.

'Just a twig,' Rawan says dismissively.

Aminah doesn't seem so sure. She's staring at the wall as if she can see through the concrete. But before I can watch the end of the play the memory starts to disappear, like a great fog has clouded over it.

I'm back at Mum's bedside again surrounded by silver branches. Right now they're shaped like a giant hand. Its gnarled fingers wrap round Mum and me as we sit in its palm, protecting us from harm.

Chapter 24

Back in primary school our whole year acted in a musical version of *Alice in Wonderland*. Elle was Alice, of course. I was cast as the Gryphon, who is only in the story for a tiny bit. Still, I was terrified, and almost didn't do it. The day before the play I cried during the rehearsal.

Mum and Dad were still together then, and they both came to watch me perform.

As I sang I remember looking out into the audience. Mum was wiping her eyes with a tissue, crying. No, she was practically sobbing.

Afterwards she hugged me tight.

'Mum,' I choked. 'You're squishing me.'

'You were wonderful, Safiya,' Mum said, sniffing.

I laughed, smiling my gap-toothed grin. 'Calm down, Mum. It was only a small part.' Secretly I was happy because Mum can be hard to please.

'Yes, but you did it beautifully, and you were very, very brave.'

I know now that she was proud because acting was something we both had in common. It was something we could share. But also it was about her past, and her friends, and everything she once knew. It was about her memories.

Mum was right: we aren't so different after all. I thought we had to act the same on the outside to be similar, but we don't. What matters is what we're like inside. And just because we don't like the same things doesn't mean we're not similar. Mum loves theatre, and I love gaming. They're worlds apart, but we love them all the same.

If you cut Mum and me open we'd be filled with the very same fire, glowing red and orange and gold.

I now have a method when it comes to figuring out the objects. As soon as I came out of the last memory I wrote down every object I saw while I was there. I even made a note of the trees, and the clothes everyone was wearing. But it's not as easy as I thought it would be.

Every time I feel like I have the game sussed it throws up another challenge. The last memory didn't really have any objects in it, nothing Mum might keep. There's the script, but I checked and Rawan said they don't have it any more. Mum doesn't either. The game has levelled up again, and I need to think outside the box. But thinking about it too much hurts my brain.

Eventually I decide to take a break from trying to figure out the next object to play a game of *Fairy Hunters*. Maybe if I clear my head it'll help me see things from a new perspective.

My room disappears into dust and is replaced by the ruined palace. But no matter how hard I try, I can't shake the thoughts of Aminah. The fire fairy I'm protecting in my game morphs into her in my mind, and no matter how many times I blink I see her.

Our wizard opponents throw spell after spell at her and I try with all my might to protect her, to stop her from dying. But there's too many of them, and too little of me.

Aminah is hit. She falls, but picks herself back up.

I trail behind, my heart thump, thump, thumping because I don't want her to get hurt.

That's when the doorbell rings, making me jump.

For a moment I hesitate. I just need a minute, one more minute. But the doorbell rings again and I lose focus entirely.

Aminah is hit, and so am I. We lose the game together.

I try to shake off the weirdness and run down the stairs. At first I think it's Dad coming back from the weekly food shop without his house keys, but then Lady starts barking aggressively, so I know it can't be him.

Unlike other dogs, who would run to the door, Lady scarpers off to the living room as soon as I get downstairs.

'Traitor,' I mutter, watching her disappear round the corner.

I answer the door, surprised to see Izzy.

'Hiiiiii?' I say, a little confused. We don't live in the olden days, we have mobile phones to communicate now. Why is she at my house? I glance at my phone to make sure I hadn't missed a message from her. Nope.

'Sorry,' she says, looking nervous. 'We weren't really sure how to explain on the phone so we . . . kind of just decided to come round.'

'We?' I ask, confused, and for a moment I think she means Elle and Abir. But it's Charlotte and Gini who hang back a little, so I didn't notice them at first.

I wonder for a moment whether I'm dreaming or in a strange memory that's not my own.

'Can we . . .' Izzy hesitates. 'Come inside?'

'Oh!' I say, snapping out of it. *Be normal, Saff.* 'Of course! Er, shall I make hot chocolate?'

There's a moment of silence, where I feel like I've asked exactly the wrong question, but then the girls' faces light up and I relax.

'Yes please!' Izzy says, speaking for the trio.

'Sorry to bother you . . .' Charlotte says as we head into the kitchen. 'We just wanted to . . . well, I suppose, talk.'

Lady waltzes in from the living room, having decided the girls aren't a threat. She looks at me approvingly, like she's trying to say 'good choice'.

I almost tell her to shut up, except I realize she hasn't actually spoken.

'Is that your dog?' Gini asks delightedly.

I turn round, looking shocked. 'What dog? I don't have a dog! Who is that?'

Gini looks up, surprised. 'But she . . . Oh!' She laughs. 'Funny.' She sits on the floor stroking Lady. I almost roll my eyes because Lady's being fully charming. Big frog eyes blinking, tongue lolling. The others laugh too and I feel weirdly elated.

The four of us end up on my bed, drinks in hand, as Charlotte nominates herself to explain why they're here.

'Izzy told us about the other night at Maccies and what you did,' Charlotte says, and she sounds so much more confident than she does at school.

As Charlotte speaks Gini watches her the way a person should look at their best friend, like she's the most special person in the world. I've never really spoken to Gini, but I've noticed lately, from photos she uploads, how close she seems to be to her family abroad. Her parents are originally from Nigeria and they go back all the time during school holidays.

I wonder if Mum and I will start going to visit Aunt Zaina and Rawan?

'I wanted to come after you,' Izzy admits, looking quite upset. 'I thought they were being awful. And the whole thing at the bike shed too . . . but I was too scared . . . I guess I . . .'

'I get it,' I say, patting her back a little awkwardly. 'It's not easy to stand up to your best friend.'

'But you did!' Izzy insists. 'Anyway, Abir's not my best friend any more . . . not after that,' she says with certainty, and she fills me in on what happened after I left.

No one really said anything; they just carried on being their mean selves. Izzy made an excuse to go home, and hasn't spoken to the others since.

'I just wanted to say thank you,' Charlotte adds, after Izzy is done. 'It was so brave of you.' Gini nods in silent agreement. 'I don't . . . I don't mind how I look. Not usually. It's just when . . .'

'People point it out to you?'

She smiles. 'Exactly.'

I understand that. I've never really had a problem with how I look either. I've always liked my imperfections because they make me . . . well . . . *me*. But when someone points them out to you as if they're something bad, you can't help but think that maybe they're right.

Soon after that talk turns to Mum, and I give them a quick update. Mum's moving her arms now, and she's off the ventilator properly. Everything's going to be OK.

While we talk, Lady's head darts back and forth between us, watching the conversation. Her tongue lolls, like she's smiling. I have all the confirmation I need: she can understand English.

Dad comes home soon after and, without missing a beat, offers us a second hot chocolate. We all gratefully accept before getting into a heated debate about the best Studio Ghibli films.

'I had no idea you watched them!' I say. Finding people who love them as much as I do feels as special as finding a rare dragon's egg.

Izzy and I are Team *My Neighbor Totoro*, while Charlotte and Gini prefer *Howl's Moving Castle*.

'You *have* to come over to my house,' Gini says passionately. 'We can watch them all back to back.'

'Gini's house is *amazing*,' Charlotte says. 'Her parents have a film room with a projector in it!'

Dad interrupts our conversation with a special treat: cheese and Marmite toasties.

'Your dad's cool,' Charlotte says when he leaves.

'The coolest,' I agree.

My laptop goes off, a notification from *Fairy Hunters*. It's instantly recognizable to anyone who plays, and sounds just like a windchime.

'No way!' Gini says, jumping up and down on my bed excitedly, spilling breadcrumbs everywhere. 'You play *Fairy Hunters* too?' She looks from me to Charlotte. 'Where have you been all our lives?' Charlotte looks equally as delighted.

'You *both* play it?'

The three of us jump around in glee for a few minutes, until we catch Izzy's confused expression.

'Oh no.' Gini shakes her head. 'Show her, someone, please.' She covers her face, as if horrified.

'Maybe next time,' Charlotte says. 'Mum's just texted to say dinner's ready soon, so we'd better eat our toasties and go. You know what she's like.' She rolls her eyes and Gini smiles. In that moment they remind me of Hana and Ib. It's like they're them, I'm Aminah, and Izzy is Rawan.

Their friendship makes me happy; it's how best friends should be together. I glance at Izzy and see she's looked up *Fairy Hunters* on her phone.

'Do you want to stay for dinner?' I ask her.

Izzy says she would love to, and texts her parents to ask.

'Please convert her while she's here,' Gini says, looking at me with such seriousness that I salute.

After they leave and Izzy and I are left alone, we talk about Elle and Abir. For the whole of secondary school I've always sat next to Elle in most of our lessons, and Izzy's sat next to Abir. But she's worried they're going to be weird with us.

'*Promise* we'll sit together?' she asks a little nervously, like she thinks I might say no. It's strange knowing I have that effect on Izzy, but I won't act the way Elle did with me. There are no leaders or followers in our friendship. We're equal.

Chapter 25

When I watch the memory for a second time, I see her.

The witch throws Aminah into the tiny room in the great big tower again. But just as she's about to lock the door she stops and looks upwards, and that's when I start climbing back up the wall.

'What was that?' Hana asks, glancing around suspiciously.

'Just a twig,' Rawan says dismissively.

I peer over to find Zaina scrambling down the slide. She rushes back towards the kitchen, disappearing inside the house.

I knew it. I knew it wasn't the cats who toppled the slide a few memories ago, because I saw something by the kitchen door. It was Zaina. She's been spying on Aminah. And I have a feeling she's the key to the next object.

Dad's made us both a cup of tea, which we drink in the kitchen while we wait for Aunt Zaina to answer the phone.

Dad's already spoken to her before, to update her on Mum's condition, so this is all normal for him. Whereas I'm trying to figure out how to introduce the memory without looking too suspicious, and somehow not freak out too much about chatting to my aunt for the first time.

Aunt Zaina doesn't answer, so we wait for a bit before trying again. I make us a second tea, while Lady keeps bringing toys to me, one after the other, like she knows I'm nervous and she's trying to make me feel better. It's because that's the sort of thing that cheers her up. I wish I was a dog sometimes. Lady's biggest stress is the fact that our neighbour's cat keeps pooping in our garden.

The phone rings, and Dad, Lady and I all jump.

'Hello?' A high-pitched voice answers in Arabic, blaring out of Dad's speaker on his phone. But the voice is older than I expected. I suppose Aunt Zaina would sound different now that she's not a child.

'Hi . . .' Dad says nervously, glancing at me. 'I have Safiya here with me.' He pauses, and I awkwardly say hello.

'Hi, James. Hello, Safiya, *habibti*,' my aunt says. She

160

pronounces my name the proper Arabic way, stressing the letter 's' so it comes out all throaty. 'How's Ami doing?' she asks, getting straight to the point and saving me from talking right away.

'Well . . .' Dad begins, and then he tells her exactly what I told the girls the other day. That Mum's getting better.

When he's done Aunt Zaina says she's looking at flights to come and visit Mum as soon as she's out of the hospital.

'And you'll come see us too, Safiya? In the summer?' Aunt Zaina asks. She's a lot calmer than her ten-year-old self, and it stops me in my tracks a little.

'Of course!' I say, excited at the prospect of seeing where Mum grew up. We could even go together, Mum and I, and visit Rawan too. That's when I ask about her, and it feels as if my heart stops while I wait for Aunt Zaina's response.

'Rawan?' she says as if the name is unfamiliar. For a horrible moment I think she's forgotten her and I won't get my answers. Then: 'Of course I remember her . . .'

My heart leaps.

'Do you remember the play Mum and Rawan acted in?' I ask excitedly.

Aunt Zaina laughs. 'Yes! Your mother would sneak off to rehearse. I was always so jealous of the way she was with Rawan. You have to understand, Safiya . . . Your mother was my best friend when I was young . . .'

My heart soars as she tells her story.

'Anyway, one day I decided to get revenge. I knew our

mother would be angry if she found out Aminah was acting in a play without telling her. She would think it was a waste of time, you see. So I took photos of your mum sneaking off with our family camera. It was a game I played. I created an investigation around your mum, like she was some sort of criminal. And the photos were evidence I compiled.'

'Do you still have them?' I ask.

'Oh no. Your mother took them after Mama found them in my room. I didn't mean for her to see them, but then they had that big fight . . .'

Dad jumps in then, before I have the chance to ask about the fight. 'So she really did have a secret hideaway?' he asks and tells Zaina his own story about the cats.

While Dad and Aunt Zaina chat, my mind drifts off to my one of *my* favourite Mum stories. You'd think it would be something big, like a trip we took together, or a birthday, but it was just a very normal cold February morning . . .

'Russia Globetrot,' Mum said to the coffee-shop barista.

'Mum!' I laughed. 'That's not your name,' I whispered, confused.

'That's a pretty name,' one of the baristas commented. She spelled it as R-A-S-H-A.

'Thank you,' Mum smiled, not missing a beat.

It was another one of the games she liked to play. Come up with the weirdest name you can think of and see if you can get away with it.

'Russia.' I scrunched up my nose. 'That's a country.'

'Well done,' Mum said sarcastically.

I laughed. 'My turn next time.'

A few weeks later, when the weather turned warmer and we got ourselves some cold drinks instead, I tried out the name 'Picklina Elfinpants', and the barista didn't even blink.

'I win!' I said triumphantly, once we sat down.

Mum shook her head, laughing. 'I'll beat you next time,' she said.

We have time, I remind myself, to make more memories.

'Thank you,' I eventually say when Aunt Zaina and Dad have finished chatting.

'You are more than welcome,' Aunt Zaina says. 'Call me again, habibti.'

As soon as the phone call is finished I make an excuse to go to Mum's flat. Because I think I know what the next object is going to be: a photograph of Rawan and Mum and the other girls from the night of their rehearsal.

I race through our neighbourhood and towards town to Mum's flat, pedalling my bike with fury.

When I get there I pull out the old photo album again, and search through it desperately, looking for the picture I need to get into the next memory. But there's nothing there.

My heart sinks, like it's falling from the clouds, ready to hit the ground, splat. But then it soars, like a bird has caught it in its beak when I look through all our old photos.

Mum holding me just after I'm born; Mum and Dad standing next to me on my first day of primary school. My eyes prickle as I sift through them all. At the aquarium with Elle on my eighth birthday; our last family holiday at the beach, Mum trying to hold her hat down as the wind threatens to snatch it away.

And my favourite: a fancy dress party for Mum's birthday. It was based on her favourite book and film, *The Wizard of Oz*. Mum went as Dorothy, Dad went as the Scarecrow, and I was the Cowardly Lion.

Except I'm not so cowardly now.

We watched the film and had a dance-off and ate her favourite food, with cake for dessert. Mum said it was the best birthday *ever*.

After I'm done with the album, I pull her copy of the book out from the shelf and stroke the cover. It's made of soft green cloth with golden lettering. I sit right there on the floor, turn to the first chapter and start reading.

Dorothy lived in the midst of the great Kansas prairies, with Uncle Henry, who was a farmer, and Aunt Em, who was the farmer's wife . . .

When I turn to the next page something flutters to the floor, like a forgotten feather.

I look down. It's a Polaroid.

When I pick it up and peer at the photo I see them: all four girls in their secret hideaway, rehearsing for their play that night. I recognize Hana's headscarf and Aminah's hair with the cloth plaited into it. Rawan is climbing up the side wall to reach Aminah, as Hana and Ib watch on, grinning.

This is it. This is the object I need to unlock the next memory!

As soon as I get home I add it to my memory box with the perfume, bracelet, cats and flyer. Each of them form a separate piece of the puzzle of Mum's past. And I'm slowly putting it together in time to save her.

Chapter 26

The house is different this time. The walls are beginning to crumble again, which doesn't make sense because Mum's getting better and I'm collecting the objects. The silver branches grow thicker, shining bright in the darkness. Their yellow flowers, which have now sprouted all over, look inky blue in this light.

The smell of the perfume is overpowering today. I follow it up, up, up to the biggest bedroom in the house. It draws me in, hypnotizing me; it clouds my thoughts and fills my mind with memories that aren't my own.

I walk over to a dressing table; it's spilling with perfume and make-up, just like Mum's. And each time the house breathes, it feels as if everything might just topple over the edge. This must be my grandmother's room.

She even has a walk-in wardrobe behind the mirror of her dressing table, and I wish I could show it to Izzy because I know she'd love it.

I walk into it, and it's like being swallowed up by a rainbow. Colourful dresses and tops with beads and glitter jump out at me, asking me to dance with them. My eyes are drawn to one in particular, because I recognize it. Mum's Arabian-style mermaid dress. The one I found in her wardrobe, the one I saw her wear years ago. Only I never knew it was my grandmother's. It glistens like hidden jewels in a treasure box, beckoning me.

'We shouldn't be in here!' Rawan says nervously, before I have the chance to reach for it.

I whip my head round to look at her. Even though I know she can't be talking to me, part of me wonders if she is. But then I see Aminah waltz into the wardrobe, and I know I'm still invisible.

'Oh, calm down, Raw,' Aminah says, rolling her eyes. 'Mama's out for the day with her sisters. She won't be back for a while,' she says resolutely. 'And anyway, didn't you say we needed costumes for the play?'

Rawan purses her lips. 'Yes, but I didn't think we were going to be stealing them . . . From what you told me, your mother sounds very scary. Not someone I want to mess with.'

Aminah ignores Rawan and starts sifting through Mama's clothes instead. 'There it is!' she says, staring right at me for a moment. But then she puts her hands through me as she brandishes the mermaid dress. 'Now, we just need to find you something . . .'

I watch Aminah as she talks to Rawan. The way she scrunches up her nose when she finds something funny; the way she waves her arms around excitedly as she talks; and the way she speaks with such confidence she could be telling you the grass is blue and the ocean purple, and you would believe her.

The two of them spend ages going through Mama's clothes, chatting about the play, and trying to think up other locations for it. Then their conversation shifts a little.

'What do *you* want to do with your life?' Aminah asks Rawan.

Rawan turns to her, frowning. 'That's a serious question.' Then she shrugs. 'I don't know. I like acting and directing. I'd love to carry on with the theatre.'

'I want to go to England . . .'

Rawan glances sideways at Aminah. 'I know, you said.'

'No, I mean, I filled out my application and everything . . . They've . . . accepted it.'

Rawan's jaw drops. 'Um . . . congratulations! Why didn't you say sooner?'

'I only found out today!'

'Wait . . . how did you get your mother to agree?'

'She . . . hasn't.' Aminah looks sheepish.

'But then how did you get permission for your application?'

'My dad signed the forms when he came back for the weekend.'

'So, you're just going to . . . leave?'

'Of course not!' The pair stop searching for clothes now and settle cross-legged on the floor. 'I will tell her, just not . . . yet.' Aminah sighs. 'She's so hard to talk to. And she has these ideas about how she wants me to act, what she wants me to do. I just don't . . .'

'Want to?' Rawan finishes the sentence for her.

'Exactly.' Aminah nods. 'She wants me to do what everyone else does, but I just want to try something different. Sounds stupid, doesn't it?'

Rawan shakes her head. 'No, it doesn't. Why else do you think I'm running a secret theatre in a hidden alleyway? Still, you need to tell her . . . She's your *mum*.'

Aminah shrugs defiantly. 'So what? It's not like we have anything in common. Sometimes I think we may as well be strangers . . .'

And, before I can hear the rest of the conversation, or watch Aminah and Rawan finish searching for their costumes, I'm pulled out of the wardrobe, out of the memory, and back to the hospital. But it's OK because I have everything

I need to find the next object.

I lean in and kiss Mum goodnight. I drink in the smell of her perfume, and imagine what it's going to be like to speak to her again.

Chapter 27

We're at Gini's house today watching a Studio Ghibli film. Charlotte was right, Gini's film projector is way cool. She has her very own games room the size of our entire living room at home – just for her!

This time we found a film we can all agree on: *Spirited Away*. We're snacking on popcorn and hot chocolate while we watch.

It's nice to have something good in my life, something that isn't about hospital visits and monitors and daily updates.

Right after I saw the last memory, I went and got the mermaid dress from Mum's flat and put it in the memory box. It's getting pretty full now. I wonder if I'm close to the end of the memories, and finally unlocking Mum's door?

I'm going to stop by the hospital on the way home. I

haven't got any time to lose, especially as the walls from the house are cracking again. I don't really understand why, though. Mum's getting better, so shouldn't the house look new? I thought it was fixed again because I was saving her.

After the film Charlotte and Gini turn to Izzy and me, looking a little nervous.

'What?' Izzy asks. 'Is this when you team up and murder me and Saff?'

I can't help but think of Aminah's comment to Rawan when she asked her to join the theatre group.

Charlotte and Gini glance at one another, and Izzy sits up, sliding away from them, spilling popcorn everywhere. 'It *is?*' Izzy turns to me, wide-eyed.

'It's OK,' I say, jumping up, 'because this is molten lava.' I hold out my mug of hot chocolate. 'And if you step closer, I'll shower you with it!'

There's a moment of silence where I worry they're all going to tease me for being stupid, the way Abir has done before. But Gini picks her popcorn up and says, 'Not if I use my super magical orb-like orbs against you!'

She throws popcorn in my direction to illustrate her point. I try to catch it in my mouth and, after about ten attempts, get one.

Everyone cheers.

'Orb-like orbs?' Izzy says afterwards, snorting. 'And what exactly do they do?'

Gini grins. 'Repel molten lava, of course.'

When we're done with our play-fight Charlotte and Gini explain why they were acting so suspicious in the first place.

'So,' Charlotte says, clearing her throat, 'Gini . . . could you?'

'Oh! Yes!' Gini jumps up, grabs a remote control, and projects a website on the wall for us all to look at.

Charlotte nods. 'Thanks. So, the creators of *Fairy Hunters* are running this competition where you have to make your own game.' She shows us the entry page and some of the details using a toy wand as a pointer. 'We found out about it a while back, but didn't have anyone we thought might want to enter with us.'

'Until now!' Gini interjects, spreading her arms wide, grinning.

Charlotte clears her throat and whispers so loudly we can all hear. 'Not yet!'

She goes on to explain that you need to enter in teams of four with a unique concept developed from scratch. You have to fill in a bunch of forms where you outline all your skills, your game concept, and examples of your work.

If your team makes it to the final, you get partnered with someone at the *Fairy Hunters* headquarters. They help you design your game, which you then present at the biggest video gaming convention of the year – this summer! The same convention I couldn't get tickets for. You're invited as a special guest, and stay in a hotel with your parents.

I imagine taking Mum, and showing her a game I made with my friends. And deep down I know she would be as proud as she was when she saw me act on stage.

'We only have a week until the deadline, but it's OK because I made a spreadsheet of the most popular games and wrote out all the things they had in common. That should make it easier for us to come up with something. If you want to join, of course.' Charlotte stops talking rather abruptly, and glances sideways at Gini. She nudges her in the arm.

'Oh!' Gini exclaims. 'Now?'

Charlotte nods vigorously.

Gini explains that she is learning to code, so she can do all the technical stuff. Charlotte can organize everything and pull the project together.

'You *have* to see her bedroom. It's so tidy, it's like a museum,' Gini teases.

Charlotte ignores her. 'We've seen some of your character drawings, Izzy, in Art, and we think you're amazing!'

'And, Saff,' Gini says, turning to me. I wonder for a moment what I might have to add to the team . . . It seems they have everything covered, and I don't really have a talent, do I? 'You always write the best stories in English! Do you think you could be in charge of the idea? We'll all help, of course. And, since you're the bravest of us all, we were sort of wondering whether you could . . . present the game if we make it to the final?'

I'm about to say no. It's what the old Saff would do. But then I think about Aminah, and how she said yes to being the lead role in the play.

I take a quick look at Izzy, who nods at me encouragingly, and answer for both of us. 'Of course!'

The panic slides off Charlotte's and Gini's faces like raindrops down a window.

'Only one problem . . .' Izzy says. 'I've never played any video games before.'

Charlotte grins. 'We can fix that!'

'But,' Gini says, holding her hand up, 'we want something in return.'

Charlotte looks confused and glances at me. I shrug, unsure of what Gini's going to ask.

'Please, please, please can you teach us how to do make-up?'

An hour later Izzy's finished all our make-up. We're done up like we're about to go to a ball, except we're crowded round Gini's laptop, the *Fairy Hunters* registration page staring back at us, trying to think up a gamer tag for Izzy.

'OK, what are some of your favourite things?' Gini asks.

'Dogs, guinea pigs, make-up, drawing, mermaids.'

Charlotte laughs.

Izzy raises her eyebrows.

'Sorry,' Charlotte says. 'I just thought of one, but it's stupid.'

'Go on,' Izzy says. 'Try me.'

'Barkiedoodle.'

Silence.

'Get out,' Gini says, pointing at the door. 'That is . . . beyond awful.'

It takes a very long time for us to settle on a name.

We try QueenofDogs, but it's taken. And MakeupandMermaids and GamesandGuineapigs are too long.

'Well, what're your gamer tags?' Izzy asks eventually.

'Mine's MythicalRogue,' I say. I always wanted to be brave enough to do things my own special Saff way. And I guess now I live up to that name.

Gini is Calypso and Charlotte is AstroGirl.

'Oh, I've got it!' Charlotte finally says. 'What about SeaPixie?'

Izzy scrunches her face. 'I like "Sea", but "Pixie" doesn't feel very me.'

We end up going through a list of words until eventually I suggest 'witch'.

'SeaWitch?' Izzy says out loud, testing the words. 'Like from *The Little Mermaid*? I love that!'

As I walk through to the reception area of the hospital some time later I think of all the ways I can make it up to Mum when she wakes up.

I'll save up all my pocket money and buy us theatre

tickets to see *Wicked*.

I'll cook her dinner every weekend and bake her a cake for her birthday.

We'll visit Kuwait together, so she can show me her house for real, and tell me all about her life.

I'll never take her for granted again.

Ever.

Chapter 28

I gasp when I see the house this time.

The cracks in the walls have grown; they start small, like at the very top of a tree, and steadily get bigger, like the large base of an oak. Gouges cluster in every corner, and the branches desperately try to hold the house together, crawling over the photo frames, wrapping themselves round the walls protectively. They wriggle like worms or fingers on a giant hand. But the house is more branch than wall now.

Flowers bloom from every corner, with all the memories I now have of Mum. But even as they bloom the house is dying. The walls have lost great big chunks, the sunlight streaming inside throwing strands of light into the foyer.

The glass table in the middle of it is cracked, and the rest of the furniture looks old, like it's been abandoned for years. The plants that create a canopy above the hallway droop, and I'm forced to push them aside to move from room to room. They look like they're bowing to me, but the truth is they're dying.

I can still hear the house's heartbeat, though it's faint. *Thump*. Pause. *Thump*. *Thump*. Pause.

I can't help but feel like the house is warning me. It's telling me that I'm running out of time to save Mum, to collect all her memories.

Despite the fact that the walls are crumbling, the door to Mum's room stays firmly shut. The wood is splintered in places once more, but only enough for me to peer through. I do, and catch my second glimpse of grown-up Mum. I had worried that, perhaps, I had imagined her there.

I step back from it before I get sucked in completely. I don't want to get sidetracked again. Who knows what might happen if I do?

I end up back in the kitchen, a trail of fallen debris leading me there. A chair in the corner of the room glows, and so I sit in it, and wait.

'Where have you been?' my grandmother demands. 'Why are you wearing my dress? And what is *that* in your hands?'

Aminah turns to Mama, clearly surprised to see her there in the middle of the night.

As she steps into the light I can see that she's wearing the mermaid dress. Except it looks far too big on her, because it belongs to her mother I suppose.

'Just outside,' Aminah says, shrugging. She's trying to act casual, but her voice is shaking.

Mama raises her eyebrows. 'Don't insult me, Aminah. You're trying to tell me you dressed up in my clothes just to go outside into the courtyard?'

Aminah nods.

It was the truth after all.

Mama steps towards her. In the harsh light of the kitchen her skin glows like a wizard whose powers are charged, ready to strike.

'Don't lie to me.' Mama's eyes are fire, and her voice is ice.

And I could swear, just then, that the branches shrivel back and hiss in fear. They slither away from Mama like snakes along the wall, leaving Aminah to fend for herself.

'I'm not!' she insists.

I want so much to tell my grandmother that Mum *is* telling the truth, just not all of it.

'What is this?' Mama asks again, snatching what was in Aminah's hands: a book of fairy tales. She opens it up and reads something on the first page. 'What does this mean? "Move to England"?'

I stand up, walk over to them, and look at the inscription myself.

'Explain,' Mama says. 'Now.' The three syllables ricochet off the walls and ring around the room like angry bells.

But Aminah doesn't speak. I'm not sure if she's too scared to talk, or if she's not sure what to say. But all too quickly Mama fills the silence.

'I found the photos in your sister's room! Did you make her hide them for you?'

'What do you mean?' Aminah looks confused, but I know exactly what Mama is talking about, because this is the argument Zaina warned me about.

Mama grabs a box from the table and shoves it into Aminah's arms.

Aminah removes the lid and looks through reams and reams of photos. Aminah and Rawan rehearsing with the others over the course of several evenings. Aminah and Rawan in their secret hideaway alone.

I lean over and look at them all too.

'I will ask you one more time, and this time no lying. Where have you been? And what does this mean?' She frowns down at the book, like it's cursed. Maybe for her it is.

Aminah sighs and tells the truth. She tells Mama about the play, and about Rawan and the others.

'Why?' Mama asks simply.

'Because I enjoy it! And I . . . I . . .' Aminah looks down at her feet. 'I want to go to school abroad.'

Mama holds her free hand out to stop Aminah from speaking, as if the very action could halt the words that have already tumbled out of her mouth. 'No,' she says, shaking her head. 'No.'

The silver branches are awake. They sway to and fro, watching over Aminah and Mama.

The pair now sit at the kitchen table, and Aminah explains everything.

There's an exchange programme. She could finish school in England and go to university there too. Her grades are good enough. More than good enough.

Mama shakes her head. 'This is ridiculous. How are you supposed to look after yourself?'

'It's a boarding school. You live with the other students and –'

'Enough,' Mama says. 'I'm not listening to this. You're not going to this school and you're not doing this play.'

'Why not?' Aminah demands, standing up all of a sudden. The chair flies backwards, bouncing across the room. 'You can't just make up rules; you need a reason for them.'

The silver branches hiss, as if they're trying to

warn Aminah.

'And you need to learn to control your temper,' Mama says, her voice just as loud.

I realize now that this is where the monster was born. Here, in this room. The silver branches try to protect the house; they surround the walls and cover the windows with their claw-like limbs, but the monster's too strong. The window breaks. Glass shatters across the room, and a great black fog surrounds Aminah and Mama, threatening to swallow them up. It's so thick I feel I might suffocate.

'Like you?' Aminah says. 'Baba has already said yes, by the way, I spoke to him.'

That seems to throw Mama off guard. 'What would he know?' she spits. 'He's never here.'

'Maybe because he doesn't want to be around you!' Aminah stomps about like she's three years old again and her favourite toy has been taken away.

'Do not speak to me like that,' Mama says. 'I've had enough of this conversation. Go to bed.'

'That's what you do, isn't it?' Aminah sneers. 'When you don't want to have a conversation you send us to bed. Well, I'm not a child. I can go to bed whenever I like. And I *will* keep acting in the play *and* go to England, no matter what you say.'

'You will not,' Mama says, though she seems to have lost her conviction. 'I know what I'm talking about . . .'

Aminah raises her eyebrows.

'Really? All *you* did was get married. You've never had a job. You haven't done anything with your life, so you want to stop me living mine.'

The light in Mama's eyes has disappeared and a sad grey cloud replaces it, like the smoke that lingers after a fire dies.

But Aminah doesn't stop there, no matter how much I try to grab on to her and tell her to. Because I've made the same mistake before . . . or, I suppose, after.

I didn't care that Mum was upset. I was too angry, so I kept pushing. And so does Aminah.

'I can't wait to go away so I never have to see you again,' she says.

Mama's crying now, and it's like cracking an egg, its shell hard and firm, only to find the soft yolk in the middle.

She opens her mouth to speak, but no words come out. Instead she sweeps past Aminah and up the stairs, her perfume, anger and hurt lingering in the room after her.

Aminah sits there triumphantly.

Fog fills the room until all I can see is black. It crawls up my nostrils, down my throat and underneath my fingernails.

When I wake up in the hospital I swear the fog hovers around Mum's bed, following me down the hall and all the way home.

Chapter 29

'Safiya!' Dad calls up the stairs.

My eyes flutter open slowly.

'I'm awake . . .' I groan, and turn to look at my phone. It's only 7 a.m. Why is he waking me up so early?

'I have a meeting I need to get to now,' he reminds me. 'Make sure to have some breakfast!'

I mumble a yes, already drifting off again.

I was up late last night working on the competition entry with the girls and we managed to get most of it done. I even came up with the idea.

A group of princesses-turned-pirates, who were all trapped in the tallest towers and guarded by dragons and goblins and witches, go on a mission to free the rest of their kind. The story begins in one particular tower, just as the main character – the latest princess to be recruited – wakes up from an eternal slumber.

When the girls ask me what the tower looks like I describe the house from Mum's memories.

When they ask about the world, I talk about sand dunes and sun, palm trees and wildflowers.

And when they ask what the main character looks like I send them a photo of Aminah when she was our age.

They all love it.

Somewhere in the distance the door slams shut, and I drift back to sleep thinking of houses and perfume and starry nights.

When I next open my eyes it's gone 8 a.m. I swear, loudly. Lady looks up at me from the bottom of the bed, scandalized.

'Sorry,' I mutter sarcastically as I jump out of bed. 'But why didn't you wake me up?'

Predictably she just stares at me and yawns. I roll my eyes at her. I hate being late for school.

I brush my teeth at lightning speed and run back to my bedroom, Lady trailing at my heels. I grab my bag, which is sitting on my bed next to my jacket, and turn to leave.

That's when I see the perfume stopper roll on the floor in front of me.

I frown and it's like the thoughts go through my head in slow motion.

I turn and see the perfume bottle has fallen out of my backpack and spilled all over my bed sheets, staining them.

The smell comes almost at once. Wood, rose and orange. It feels as if the magic inside the bottle has been released, like a caged bird finally set free.

'No!' I scream.

Lady runs up to me and sniffs at the wasted perfume. I shove her aside and pick up the bottle. It's gone. I scream and scream until my throat feels sore.

Lady whimpers from the corner of the room.

The monster stirs inside me and my whole body shakes. It feels stifling in here, like it's taken over entirely, possessed the house. It's angry.

I hurry out, but after I leave the house I realize that my feet are taking me in the direction of the hospital instead of school, and soon I'm standing in front of the great ugly building, perfume still in hand.

If I see Mum now I know she'll still smell of the perfume, and I can visit the game again before it's too late.

But you need to get the book of fairy tales, Saff! And you're not ready for that, are you?

I try to bite down the panic that's expanding inside me.

Before I know it I'm there, outside Mum's hospital room. I don't remember going up in the lift or walking through the doors. It's like there's a gaping black hole in my mind.

I see a bunch of doctors and nurses surrounding Mum's bed, including Amanda and the doctor that always chats to Dad.

My heart leaps. What's wrong? What are they doing?

I watch as they talk. They seem serious, very serious.

The machine is making all sorts of noises, and they're mumbling things I can't hear.

Amanda sees me. She mutters something to the doctor, who looks over at me before turning back to Amanda with a curt nod, and jogs towards me.

'Safiya?' Amanda says. 'Shouldn't you be in school?' She glances in the direction of the empty reception desk with a frown. I suppose someone should have been there to stop me getting in.

I ignore her question. 'Why are they sticking things in her mouth . . . and . . .' My voice breaks.

'All right,' Amanda says soothingly. 'Let's go over here, shall we?' She talks to me like I'm a scared animal, and leads me to an empty office down the hall.

'What's happening?' I ask as soon as the door shuts behind us.

I try to settle into the giant armchair that sits across from Amanda. The size of it makes me feel like I'm little again.

Last year me and Elle went back to our old primary school, where her mum works. We helped her set up her classroom for World Book Day. All the desks seemed tiny, the rooms too.

'I think it's best for the doctor to discuss it with your father . . .' Amanda says cautiously. 'Sometimes there are just –' she sighs – 'complications . . .' Her sentence fizzles out. It seems she's stuck for words, like she's holding something back.

We talk for a while, but it doesn't help. My chest feels like it's weighed down by rocks and I'm sinking down, down, down towards the bottom of the ocean.

A cleaner comes in just then, interrupting our chat. 'Sorry,' he says, looking between us, before shutting the door behind him.

'Are you OK now, Safiya?' Amanda asks, eyeing up my uniform. 'Do you think it might be a good idea to go to school? Get your mind off things?' She looks troubled. 'Your dad does know you're here, doesn't he?'

No.

I nod. 'Can I see her?'

'Not right now, love. But we'll be chatting to your dad soon. Maybe you can come in with him and see her later?'

Another nod.

As I leave, it takes everything I have to concentrate on walking. Left and right, my legs feel tingly and weak. Eventually I make it out of the hospital, but I don't walk in the direction of school.

Ten minutes later I'm letting myself into Mum's flat. I dump my stuff down, collapse on to the sofa, and burst into tears.

Chapter 30

I dream that the house is filling up with water. I'm at one end of it and Mum's at the other. She's awake, and we try to swim towards each other. But just as we are about to grab each other's hands, seaweed wraps round my feet, like slimy fingers, and pulls me back.

I try again and again. Each time I get a little bit closer and I grab on to her tighter, but I can never get close enough.

Eventually the seaweed has wrapped itself round my entire body, like a caterpillar's cocoon, and I can barely see Mum any more, barely see anything.

I call out her name, but no sound comes out. My voice is lost in the bubbles.

*

We're in Dr Oriji's office later in the day, the same office Amanda took me to just a few hours ago. I sit in the same chair, but it doesn't seem big this time. It seems just right, like I've grown up far more than I should have in the last few hours. Like I'm growing as the conversation ticks on.

I feel groggy from the events of the morning and my eyes are still swollen from crying.

'We're going to run some tests,' Dr Oriji explains.

The doctor sounds like she's speaking in slow motion. I watch her lips form the words that make my stomach twist in knots. And when she's done it's like everything is moving in double speed to catch up.

'What sort of tests?' Dad asks, frowning. We agreed that I would come in today, that I needed to know, but Dr Oriji looks at me nervously, like she doesn't want to say the next words in front of me. She opens her mouth, then closes it, rubbing her chin with her forefinger and thumb. Eventually she settles, arms resting on her desk.

'We're testing for brain stem death,' she explains.

Death. Death. Death.

The word thumps in my mind like something slamming hard against my skull until I bury my face in my hands. It doesn't go away, and I want to scratch at my skin, my hair, to get it out. But it's too rooted inside me to simply pluck out, and all I can do is cry.

There's a bit of fumbling while Dr Oriji gets me a tissue, and Dad pulls his chair closer to mine. He holds my hand while the doctor continues to explain.

Apparently Mum is no longer in a normal coma – the one where you think the person might wake up. The complications mean that they have to check her brain function to make sure that everything's working. And they've put Mum on the ventilator again, so she's not breathing on her own any more.

But I know her brain is working. I've been swimming in her memories as I've played the game. How could all this be happening if she isn't alive?

Because you spilled the perfume. You ruined the game.

I push the thoughts aside and focus instead on what I can do to fix things.

I tried to look up the perfume, but nothing came up in my search. I suppose there are no 'magical perfume' shops online.

All that's left in the bottle is the oily residue, barely enough for a drop.

What if I dilute it? That way it can last a bit longer.

Yes! I think. Just enough to finish the game.

I'm getting closer, I can feel it.

Dr Oriji's voice shatters through my thoughts of the past and catapults me back to the present moment with the force of an elastic band.

The doctors will run a series of tests. They're a bit weird and oddly simplistic, like those science experiments you do in primary school, but on a human. They do each of the tests twice with two different doctors. The doctors then meet to discuss the results.

When I ask Dr Oriji how often this happens she says it's standard procedure for this sort of thing. When I ask her what happens if Mum fails all the tests, she doesn't give me a straight answer, just looks at Dad.

But that tells me everything I need to know. If Mum fails the tests, then it's GAME OVER.

My limbs feel heavy whenever I move, like someone's tied rocks to them to weigh me down. It's like everything happening in my life is a bad dream, and I have to shake myself awake every few moments. Somehow it's the memories that feel most real to me now.

'Do you want to visit your mum?' Dad asks, but his voice sounds far away.

I nod, even though I don't have the book of fairy tales to unlock the next memory. Elle has it, but I'm not ready to face her just yet.

Today I want to see Mum and spend time with her without worrying about having to solve puzzles. So, I forget about memories and games and tests; I just sit by her bedside, pull *The Wizard of Oz* from my bag, and read.

Chapter 31

I ring Elle's doorbell three times before someone answers. While I wait I'm not quite sure what to do with my hands so I swap from clasping my hips, to crossing them in front of me. It looks like I'm doing a weird version of the hokey-cokey.

Eventually I stick my hands in my jacket pocket and play with the perfume bottle. I brought it and the bracelet with me. They're my weapon and armour as I face the next challenge of the game.

Years ago, on my tenth birthday, Mum gave me a book of fairy tales. Except I wasn't really into that sort of thing. I had just started playing video games and all I wanted was a new console. I never even looked in it, just gave it to Elle, because she was obsessed with princesses at the time.

If I had bothered to read it, maybe I would have asked

Mum who 'R' was, and I would have known everything I know about her now sooner.

I hope Elle hasn't given the book away. What'll I do if I can't get the next object?

'Safiya!' Elle's mum says when she opens the door, obviously startled to see me. I wonder if Elle told her we don't sit together at school any more. 'I . . . Elle's around somewhere. Let me get her.'

'Hey,' Elle says, equally surprised, when she sees me.

I want to ask for the book and leave as soon as I can, but I don't think that's the point of the challenge. When I found the cats I ended up talking to Dad about Mum; when I found the flyer for the play I started emailing Rawan; and after I spoke to Aunt Zaina she agreed to visit. So, I know today I have to do this properly.

'Can I come in?' I ask.

When we get to Elle's room it's like travelling back in time. She has pink and white striped wallpaper and pink glittery curtains to match. Her room's been like this since she was seven.

'Mum's going to redecorate,' Elle says, as if she's embarrassed, when she sees me looking around. I realize I haven't been here in a while.

'Really?' I frown. 'I like it how it is.'

Elle shrugs and flops on to her bed. 'Want a drink?' she asks like nothing's changed.

I shake my head. Silent Saff is back again, and I'm

not quite sure how to start the conversation. I don't feel awkward, though, not this time. I just wait for Elle to speak because I think she owes me that.

Eventually she does.

'How's your mum?' she asks, looking concerned. 'Is she still in a coma?'

I can feel my blood boil as the words leave her mouth. Even though she looks like she cares, she asked about Mum in the same way you'd ask someone if they watched a popular programme on TV, or finished their homework on time.

'Yes, she is,' I snap. 'What kind of question is that?'

'Sorry,' Elle answers, eyes wide. She's not used to me being mad at her.

'She's going to be fine,' I add, though I'm not sure who I'm trying to convince.

There might've been a time when I would've told Elle about Aminah and Rawan and the challenges I've had to face. For some reason, though, I don't, even though she's acting like things are normal.

Maybe because I'm not sure she would believe me. Maybe because I'm not sure she's special enough to share this with any more. Seeing Rawan and Mum together makes it clear how much things have changed between Elle and me.

Elle says nothing in response.

'Anyway,' I carry on, taking charge now, 'do you

remember that book of fairy tales I gave you?' I describe it for her when she looks confused.

I watch Elle's brain tick, my heart pounding. She doesn't have it, I knew it!

'Oh!' Elle finally says. 'Do you mean this?' She rummages at the very back of her cupboard. She doesn't even have it on her bookshelf.

It's dusty, and there's a mark on the cover that didn't exist when Mum gave it to me. It might just be a book to Elle, like all the other ones she has, but it's special to me. It *means* something. And right now I wish I had never given it away.

'You can have it back,' Elle says, like I let her use my hairbrush. 'That reminds me! Can I borrow your boots this weekend? Matty's taking me to a trampoline park, so I need something comfy.'

'Um . . . I guess,' I say.

'Awesome. Sit next to each other on Monday, yeah? Then I can tell you all about it.'

I don't respond or say that I quite like sitting next to Izzy and spending lunch with Gini and Charlotte. This always happens with Elle. She gets annoyed at me and I wait for her to stop being mad. But things are different this time, I just don't know how to say that.

I say my goodbyes then, and Elle waves me off from her bed. As I make my way into the hallway I notice the stained-glass window that looks out into Elle's perfect garden. But instead of grass and apple trees and sun, it transforms into sand and palm trees and stars.

Mum and Rawan are sitting together. They're laughing about something I can't hear, sharing sugar sweets and drinking tea like they always do. The two cats loiter around them, probably hoping for scraps. Eventually the cats settle, the heart-shaped markings on their backs align, tails twisting together.

Come on, Saff, I whisper to myself. *You can do this.*

And that's when I turn back to Elle.

I take a deep breath and, for the first time in our entire friendship, I speak my mind.

'Things changed this year,' I begin, pausing while I gather my thoughts. 'I thought it was my fault at first, and that I was being a bad friend.

'I thought I wasn't growing up quick enough. I couldn't understand why I didn't care about boys. I thought it meant I was being selfish and jealous and silly . . . then I realized *I'm* not the problem,' I say with certainty.

'OK,' Elle eventually says, stretching out her vowels. 'I mean, I sort of get it.'

'You do?' I raise my eyebrows, not convinced.

Elle nods. 'Me and Abir were talking about this actually. We think that maybe *we're* the ones who are growing up a bit quicker. But we can't really help it, you know? It's just . . . we're more mature, I guess. You'll get there eventually.' She smiles, like she's being helpful and not mega patronizing.

'Like the games and cartoons. Maybe when you grow out of all that, other things will replace it. But you're right. It's not your fault. It's just . . .' She shrugs, not finishing her thought.

It's just that I'm better than you. I know it's what she's thinking.

Elle's wrong, so wrong. Liking games and animated films doesn't make me immature – it means I have interests. But letting your friends get picked on by means boys *is*. And anyway, who says being mature has anything to do with fancying people? Not everyone has to fancy someone. Not ever, if they don't want to.

But I don't say any of that – I just say the one thing that needs to be said. 'I don't think we can be friends any more,' I announce, and it's like butterflies are swarming in my belly. But then they fly out of my mouth and out of the window to where Rawan and Aminah are sitting in the garden. And that's when I leave Elle's room for good, the monster trailing behind me.

It followed me home the day Aminah and Mama had their argument. It sits in the corner of my room and follows me around, waiting for the right moment to strike. Except it's not a monster at all: it's a shapeshifter. And today it's a fairy.

Sometimes the shapeshifter is angry and hurtful, but other times it's kind and passionate. That's the thing about having fire inside you the way Mum and I do: once you learn to control it, it's like having the best superpower around.

As I walk out of Elle's house towards the hospital I put the perfume bottle back in my bag for safe-keeping. I take a glance back towards Elle's garden, but the desert oasis has disappeared, replaced by neat hedgerows and flowers.

I think back to primary school, Elle in front, me following, as we formed a snake in the playground. Today I finally broke the link.

I don't need Elle to lead me any more. Because I can lead myself.

Chapter 32

Before I enter Mum's hospital room, I stop by the water filter, and pull the perfume bottle from my bag. My hands start shaking as I fill it with a drop of water, then two. Just enough.

I give the bottle a sniff. It's diluted, but the smell is still there.

One drop. Two drops. Three.

They slide and sink into her skin like always. And it's as if, in that moment, the magic has been unlocked.

The room starts to fade. I can no longer feel the hard chair I'm sitting on, or the hospital floor beneath my feet. I can no longer hear the ventilator, or the nurses chatting in the corridor. For a moment it's as if I don't exist. And then all at once I'm back there, in the house.

An enormous rug stretches across the living room, embroidered in blues and greens, but it's worn, half the thread spilling out of it, resembling an tumultuous ocean. A diamond chandelier hangs over the rug, cracked, its ends jagged, like stars twinkling in the sky.

This is the room where I first met Aminah. I think back to her argument with Zaina and Mama, and then I think about how much their lives have changed, how much my life has changed.

The room is the size of my entire house put together. The furniture is covered in all sorts of patterns, and there are antique cabinets with items made of gold that glisten. But a layer of dust has settled over everything like it's been empty for years, waiting to be found. Waiting to be searched.

I cross the rug and look up at the chandelier. One of the cracked diamonds winks at me, like it's asking me to choose it. I drag an ornate chair across the room, though its arm is now hanging off, broken, and place it just beneath the diamond. I climb the chair and prise it off. As soon as my fingers clasp round it, the room erupts into chatter.

Dozens of women wearing colourful Kuwaiti-style dresses – pink, orange and green – stand around the room talking. The men wear traditional clothes too as they huddle together in one corner around a hookah, a cloud of smoke enveloping them. Children rush from one side of the room to the other, chasing one another.

A great big platter of food stands at the centre of the room – it holds melon, tea, dates, and elaborate sugar sweets piled up in a great big tower.

It must be Eid. Mum told me about it once and it sounded exactly like this.

I scan the crowd, trying to spot her. Then I see her dashing down a hallway that leads out from the living room to an exit I haven't seen before.

I fling myself off the chair and follow. As I cross the room my brain tunes in to all the different conversations spoken in both Arabic and English. The smell of even more food travels up from the kitchen; it makes my mouth water. But everything else fades into the background as I follow Aminah through a narrow archway. This one is lined with green plants, just like the others, the yellow flowers blooming. But they're not drooping this time; they're very much alive.

It must be because I'm in a memory, I think. The entire house looks whole again, and I wish it would stay like this forever.

Aminah exits through a back door that leads to a staircase outside.

The warmth hugs me like an old friend, and I breathe it in, welcome it.

You can see the entire neighbourhood from here, past

the gate: the park across the street and the corner shop, Rawan's house next door, and the others that line the street. Lights shine from each of their windows, like open eyes, watching. I can see the edge of the game too. It's hazy, like everything beyond it is a mirage. I remember first coming into it, and everything falling apart as I tried to leave.

The two cats wander the courtyard, sniffing around for scraps of food.

At the top of the steps sits a woman looking out at the neighbourhood like a queen watching over her people. It takes some time for my eyes to adjust, and then I see it's Mama.

Aminah sits down next to her. They sit in silence for some moments, staring up at the sky together, just as the call to prayer starts.

A throaty voice echoes across the neighbourhood. A millisecond later another voice joins it from a nearby mosque, then another. All throughout the country the same words can be heard at the exact same moment, each additional voice adding strength so they speak as one. The wind picks up pace just then and it's as if the voices have caused it from their collective prayer. It's as if the sound of their words make the pebbles in the street leap and the leaves on the trees quiver. Together they bring the people to a halt, and all of Kuwait is silent. The sound echoes through the country, so powerfully it seems as if it could reach the moon, even the stars. And when it's done, the wind halts too.

'Can you see a tiger?' Mama asks when the prayer falls silent.

Aminah turns to her, frowning. 'Where?' she asks, following her mum's line of sight. 'In the sky?'

'Yes, look.' Mama angles Aminah's face so she's looking just so.

Aminah laughs. 'No, but I think I can see a heart shape. Aren't you supposed to do this with clouds?'

Mama smiles. 'But we never have any clouds,' she says simply. 'Isn't it interesting how we never see the same thing? Your brain connects different dots to mine. It's all about the way we see the world.'

Aminah nods. 'That's true.'

'Tiger and heart.'

'Tigerheart.' Aminah grins. 'Sounds good, doesn't it?'

'Maybe you can name your theatre company that.' Mama turns to her and, with that, something in the conversation shifts.

Aminah looks at her mother in surprise. 'You're going to let me act in the play?'

Mama says nothing, only smiles, and it's like a hundred stars shining all at once.

'Mama, I –'

'Darling I –' Mama says at the same time.

Silence descends.

Mama speaks again. 'I want to tell you a story . . . A long

time ago, when I was your age, I wanted to go to America. I never asked my parents, of course, but they knew of my obsession. I wanted to be a singer, like Ella Fitzgerald. She was a bit before my time but I loved her music. I still do. Anyway, one day my parents called me down. They had an announcement for me. I thought they were going to tell me we were going to America, or maybe they were going to send me to singing lessons . . .'

Mama falls silent, playing with the gold bangles wrapped round her wrist.

'What happened?' Aminah eventually asks, inching closer to her mother.

Mama smiles, looking at Aminah. 'You'll find out one day soon, though I'm afraid the story doesn't have a happy ending.' Aminah frowns. 'But I am telling you this because I want you to do whatever it is you want with your life, even if that means moving away.'

Mama says nothing more. Instead she takes Aminah's hand and leads her back through the Eid celebrations. She leads her up the stairs and to her room, all the while holding her hand. Aminah's other hand hangs loosely by her side, the bracelet round her wrist, and I pretend to hold on to it too.

When they get to Mama's room she lets go of Aminah's hand and reaches for her dressing table. She pulls out a purple bottle made of glass cut into the shape of a diamond, a golden heart-shaped stopper at the top. Just like the one in my pocket.

'What's this?' Aminah asks.

'Perfume, of course,' Mama says. 'But not just any perfume; this one is special. With each year that passes the smell of the perfume will grow stronger, more fragrant. Try to save it for as long as you can. It will age with you. And knowing you, it will get better with each year.'

That's when I understand Mama's words. *You'll find out one day soon.* She means through her memories . . . Has this all happened before?

Aminah hugs her mother then, and I step closer to them both, inhaling Mama's perfumed scent. It's overpowering, stronger than I've ever smelled it before.

'I'm sorry,' Mama says. 'I want you to make your own choices. I want you to perform in the play, go to school wherever you want. I want the world to be open to you, not a closed book.' Her voice shakes a little as she finishes speaking. 'Like mine has been.'

'I'm sorry too!' Aminah declares.

And the memory fades as the two of them say 'I love you'.

I don't hear the rest of their conversation; I don't know how Mama's story ends. But I suppose that's for Aminah to find out.

Everything becomes hazy then, like a fog has descended over Mum's mind.

The perfume's running out, even though I diluted it. But that's OK because I just need one more memory to finish the game.

The perfume is the object that brought me into this world, and it's the final object I need to complete the memory box.

Now all I need to do is unlock the door and wake Mum up.

Now all I need to do is save her.

And I know where I'm going to get more perfume . . .

Chapter 33

Charlotte: Hey, girls! I've just sent our competition entry. We should hear back soon!

Gini: I'm so excited! And scared.

Izzy: I've just levelled up on *Fairy Hunters!*

Saff: Yay, Izzy!

Gini: Ha ha. How much are you playing it?

Izzy: No comment. Mum's already yelled at me once when I refused to come down for dinner.

Charlotte: UGH. Parents don't understand that if you leave halfway through a game you get banned.

Gini: Oh yeah! Thanks for the cool name, Saff.

Izzy: YES. Team Tigerheart. I love it!

I have another plan up my sleeve: my bed sheets. When I spilled the perfume it leaked all over my bed. My entire room smells like wood and rose and orange. Maybe that's why I'm seeing Aminah everywhere. The perfume is part of my blood now. If I just take the bed sheets to the hospital with me . . .

And that's when there's a knock on my door.

Dad lets himself into my room, which he *never* usually does. At first I think it's because he's telling me Mum's woken up. But then I see his expression, and it makes me stop in my tracks.

'What is it?' I ask him, knowing that it's something big.

'Can I sit down?' Dad asks.

'What is it?' I repeat. I can't bear to wait.

The seconds that pass feel like an age, and it's like Dad's next words are spoken hours later, like I could fit a whole lifetime into those seconds.

'I've just been on the phone with the hospital.' I'm glued to my computer chair while he perches on my bed. I don't want to get closer to him for some reason, like that'll make what he's about to say more real. 'They've . . . given us an update.' His voice cracks and that's when time speeds up, like I'm watching everything in fast forward. 'They haven't confirmed – they can't over the phone – but I wanted to tell you before we go that it's . . . it's not going to be good.' The word 'good' is barely a whisper. Dad's face crumples and he cries.

I stand up to go to him but my legs buckle and I'm on the floor. I open my mouth to say something, to cry out, but nothing happens.

A tingling sensation starts from the tips of my fingers right up my arms. Then it moves to the tips of my toes right up my legs. The sensations meet at the very centre of my belly where the monster lives. It wakes and roars, but it's different today, defeated. When it stops all I am is a hollow pit where fire once burned. I feel like Alice crying silently while the room fills up with my tears.

Dad says something but it sounds muffled. The tears reach my bed and I'm dunked into water, sinking down, down, down.

Dad's arms wrap round me but instead of feeling comforted I feel strangled, like a snake is trying to squeeze all the air from my body. My chest feels heavy and I'm drowning.

I pull away from him and huddle up by my bed frame, knees against my chest, face buried into my knees.

The water has reached the top of my window now. It swallows everything up whole and all that's left is smoke and ash where I once stood.

Chapter 34

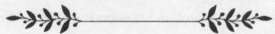

I don't leave my bed until the next evening when Dad convinces me to have a bath. I don't go to school or reply to any of the messages from Izzy, Gini and Charlotte asking me if everything's OK. I play with the bubbles, letting the warmth of the water seep into my bones.

Tomorrow we will go see the doctors, and they're going to tell us it's GAME OVER. That's what Dad said.

So now, all I can do is wait. Strangely, though, that doesn't feel right. I can't just give up, can I? Once, in *Fairy Hunters*, my health was down to four per cent. I had three wizards zapping spells at me, but I still managed to win. I even got a special mention for it on the message board. If I did it once, maybe I can do it again!

Something hums in my belly, like a swarm of bees on a mission. It works its way up, up, up until I absolutely have to see Mum.

I need to at least try to save her, don't I? I can't give up yet!

I just need the final object: the perfume. I know it has to be that because Mama gave it to Mum in the last memory.

I jump out of the bath, water splashing everywhere. With my favourite PJs on I run into my room. But something's different. My bed sheets have been changed. Instead of yellow stars they're covered in pink flowers. My room has been tidied too, all while I've been in the bath. I can no longer smell the perfume, all I can smell are the hot chocolate and cheese and Marmite toasties sitting on my bedside table.

No. No. No.

I run down to the laundry basket, which sits just off the kitchen, and pull everything out. They're not there.

'What are you looking for Saff?' Dad asks, peering at me from the living room. 'Did you have a nice bath?'

Lady runs up to me and sniffs all the discarded clothes on the floor.

'Where are my bed sheets?' I demand.

'On your bed,' Dad says, obviously confused.

I scowl. 'Not those!' I snap. 'Where are the starry ones?'

'In the wash.' He nods at the washer, which is on right now.

My eyes widen. In between the swirling water and bubbles are my starry bed sheets, the perfume washing out of them and down the drain.

'What have you done?' I yell and it's as if the fire has ignited in my belly again. But this time it's dangerous, like it might spread too far and burn down an entire forest.

Dad frowns. 'I changed your bed sheets,' he answers. I never yell at him. Ever. 'Saff, are you OK? Did you want to talk about –'

'No!'

And then I grab the memory box from my room and bolt out of the house.

'Saff!' I hear Dad calling me. 'Saff!'

By the third call I can no longer hear anything but my heart thudding in my head.

When I get to Mum's flat, after twenty minutes of furious biking, I rush to her bedroom again.

I can smell it, smell the perfume as clear as I could weeks and weeks ago.

I tear all the clothes from her wardrobe until I find her favourite jacket. The smell is overpowering.

With the bracelet round my wrist, the now empty perfume bottle in the pocket of Mum's jacket, and the memory box in my arms, I run the rest of the way to the hospital, abandoning my bike.

I can see the hospital building at the end of a narrow path, and I feel like Dorothy as she crosses the poppy field to get to Oz.

When I finally make it to the ward I realize with horror

that the scary nurse, Sue, is on the reception desk again and visiting hours are over for the day. But I won't let her stop me. She's like the dragon guarding the princess in the tallest tower. Or the witch locking her up and throwing away the key.

I wait until Sue has her back turned and, like something out of a movie, spider-crawl across the floor until my back is up against the desk. She's back at her computer after a few moments, tap, tap, tapping, and that's when it hits me.

I bury my face in my hands. This is ridiculous, I'm ridiculous. I wait for an age, frozen to the spot, staring at Mum's door. If I stretched my legs out I might even reach it. But Sue would see me.

Suddenly I hear a door open and shut and someone breathes in sharply. I close my eyes, waiting for her next words. 'Excuse me, what are you doing out of –' Her steps clip-clop in time with her words, each one like a slap. 'You're not a patient.'

That's when Sue stands up. I hear her chair roll away. 'What are you on about?' She sounds irritated.

I stand up too and Sue jumps backwards. I would find that funny if I wasn't so upset. 'I . . . I just wanted to see my mum.'

Sue's eyes widen and it looks like they might pop out of her head entirely. The other nurse's expression changes and she puts her hand on my arm. 'Where's your mum, darling?'

She asks this just as Sue says, 'Visiting hours are over.'

I don't know what comes over me, but I burst into tears. 'S-she's in there and I w-want to t-talk to her.' They're both distressed by my crying. Sue is shushing me, obviously worried that I'll bother the patients. The nice nurse leads me behind the desk and sits me down on an empty chair.

Even as I realize how silly I must look to them, I can't stop.

I hear the two whispering for a moment before Sue picks up the phone and resumes her work. I tune her out. The nice nurse comes over soon after with a grey-looking cup of tea in a cardboard cup. 'Thank you,' I say, tears still streaming down my face.

'Your mum's Aminah, isn't she?' The nurse asks with a smile. She has crooked teeth and blond hair tied up in a bun. There are faded pink streaks in it that show when the light is just right.

I nod and, before I know it, I'm telling her all about Mum's memories, and showing her the items from the memory box.

'That dress is beautiful!' the nurse says, stroking it like it's a fragile puppy or kitten.

Sue huffs occasionally as we speak; the nice nurse rolls her eyes and we grin at one another. It's a relief to go over it, and the nice nurse looks engaged, her eyes sparkling as I talk.

'Wow,' the nice nurse says when I'm done. 'I've always

wanted to go to –'

'Safiya?'

I turn round. 'Dad?' I say, surprised.

He looks old for his years, his face a canvas of wrinkles. My heart aches to see it. Were they there before all of this?

The nice nurse leads me to him and I thank her.

'Dad,' I whimper, falling into his arms. 'It's all my fault.'

Dad frowns. 'What is?'

'All of it!' I sob, and then I tell him.

I tell Dad about the argument and the horrible things I said; I tell him about all those times I pushed Mum away, and how I never listened; then I tell him about the headache she had, and how I kept pushing things, even though she felt bad.

By the time I'm done Mum's jacket is covered in my tears, and the nurse has made two trips to get me tissues.

'Safiya,' Dad says, pulling me aside so we have privacy. 'Look at me,' he says, and I do. I stare into his big blue eyes until I feel grounded again. Because right now it's like I'm made of helium, and I could float, float, float away into the sky. 'This is not your fault. None of it is.'

He goes on to explain that Mum was sick long before our argument; she just didn't know it.

'But –'

Dad holds his hand up. 'I'm not finished,' he says warmly, using the same hand to stroke my cheek. 'Your mother loves you,' he says. 'More than *anything*. And an argument, no matter how big, isn't going to change that.'

'But . . . but I never said it.' My lip quivers.

'Said what?'

'I love you.'

Dad shakes his head and laughs. 'You don't need to say it, Safiya. She already knows.'

Does she? I think. *Does she really?*

Dad must sense my doubts. 'Weren't you the one who painted Mum's new flat with her?'

I nod.

'And didn't you dress up for her birthday and plan a party?'

I nod again.

'And what about that time you walked from town with her favourite coffee and breakfast to make her feel better when she was ill?'

I had forgotten this, all of it.

'OK. So don't be so hard on yourself. You did your best.'

I wish his words could fix this, but I'm not sure they can. Still, they're grounding me. But that's Dad: he always stops me from floating away into the stars.

'Now, what's that you have there?'

I look down at the memory box. I got some wrapping paper that looks like a map of the world and stuck it to the outside of the box and lid. I thought Mum would like it. I lift the lid and show Dad all the objects.

'Been on a scavenger hunt, have you?' he asks, his voice

breaking. Tears slide down his face as he sifts through the items.

I explain how I wanted to be closer to her.

'Shall we go and see her one more time before we meet the doctors?'

I nod, not trusting myself to speak any more.

Dad explains to the nurses that we need to see Mum, and they let us into her room just for a few minutes. He holds my hand as we enter, squeezing it tight.

'It's OK, Saff,' Dad says, my steady rock in a choppy ocean. 'It's going to be OK.'

Chapter 35

When I was little my parents took me to horse riding club. I think they were worried because I was really shy back then, and they wanted me to learn to talk to people. I would clean the stables and feed the horses and help fetch equipment for lessons.

I loved the club for a while, until one day a horse bucked me off its back. I fell, *splat*, into the mud and broke my arm. After it healed Mum took me back and told me I had to get on the horse again. The same one. But my legs wobbled like jelly, and I cried and screamed and clung on to her shirt.

'Safiya,' she said, bending to my height, 'you and me, we're the same. We have fire in our belly and we can do anything. Being brave is about doing something even when it scares you.'

I sniffed, my face covered in tears, and I got on the horse.

Nothing bad happened that time.

On the way home Mum bought me an ice cream. 'I'm proud of you, my little girl,' she said. 'You're the bravest.'

I've been hiding from the world for the last week now. We met with the doctors and they've diagnosed Mum with 'brain stem death'. They're switching off her ventilator next week, which means she'll stay asleep forever. Like a real princess in a tower.

Dad talked to the school and they agreed to let me have a couple of weeks off. I've spent most of my days casting spells and defeating wizards in the world of *Fairy Hunters*, and living off cheese and Marmite toasties. Lady's thrilled because she has a friend with her at all times, and she follows me around like a shadow. But I'm glad for it, because I don't know what I would do without her.

I keep crying over random things. Like the other day I went to make a toastie, but we were out of Marmite, so I burst into tears. Dad rushed in and, as soon as he saw what was wrong, he went to the shop and bought three jars and an extra big tub of hot chocolate.

The girls have been messaging me non-stop, but I've been ignoring them. Then, Izzy sends me the most special message I've ever received.

Izzy: I know things are hard for you at the moment, but we just want you to know we're here for you. You don't have to talk about it or anything, but we thought you might like to see this . . .

I open the attachment and, as I look at what she's sent, my heart stirs, like a bear on the first day of spring.

Staring at me, from my computer screen, is a drawing of Aminah. She's dressed in a hybrid princess-pirate outfit, sword in hand. And she's standing in front of the ruined house. A darkness, like tar, tries to reach for her. It looks like a shadow dragon barricading the door to stop her from going in, but she's ready to fight. The two cats position themselves behind her, her accomplices, ready to help.

My eyes fill up with tears, happy tears. But they're also sad, because it's Mum.

Lady scratches at my bedroom door, whining for me to let her in because I accidentally locked her out. When I do she sniffs round my feet excitedly, like she can sense the change in me.

I suddenly have the urge to be closer to Mum. I'm not ready to visit her at the hospital again, but I have another place I can go. The place where this all started: Mum's flat.

Fifteen minutes later I have my coat on and Lady is bouncing up and down next to me. 'Going for a w-a-l-k,' I say, peering into the living room, where Dad's busy working. I have to spell the word because Lady understands when I say 'walk', but I'm pretty sure she knows how to spell since she's now glued to my side, almost tripping me up whenever I try to move. There's also the fact that I'm holding her lead, ready to clip it on to her. That *might've* given it away.

Dad looks up, his reading glasses magnifying his eyes. 'With Lady?'

I nod. 'I need the fresh air.' I almost leave it at that, but I decide to tell him. 'And I'm going to Mum's flat.'

'OK,' Dad says, his eyes lingering on me as I turn on my heel. 'Love you.'

I turn back. 'Love you too,' I say, because I don't want to ever forget those words again.

When I get to Mum's flat I let Lady off her lead so she can explore.

There's a load of post by the door, official-looking envelopes that I put aside for Dad. I add the rest to the existing pile. That's when I notice the delivery note again, the one I saw on my very first visit. The note says a package has been left with the next-door neighbour.

Curious, I run across the hall and knock. And I can't help but think how the old Safiya would never be brave enough to do this.

The woman who lives in this flat is much older than Mum. She's friendly, even though we don't know her very well.

'Oh yes! I've got it out back,' she says, when I show

her the delivery note. Then she retreats into her flat, the door wide open. She's wearing a kaftan-style dress and a headband.

I peer over her shoulder to see a burst of colour and patterns. Fabric lines the walls and the faint smell of cat litter lingers, masked by incense.

As if it knows its cue a three-legged fluffy grey cat jogs to the door. It lets out a small sharp miaow. I can't tell if it's greeting me or telling me to leave, but soon it rubs its body all over my legs and I know I'm welcome.

The incense wafts towards me and I'm reminded of the monthly ritual Mum performed with her *bakhoor*, and the bird in the game that led me to Aminah's bedroom.

'Sorry about her,' the woman says, nodding at her cat, as she returns with a package.

I smile. 'Oh, that's fine. Thank you.'

When I get back to the flat Lady sniffs at me suspiciously. She looks up at me all upset, and I can read the words in her eyes: *traitor*, she says.

Eventually she lets out a sound between a snuffle and a snort, and trots back to the foot of the armchair. That was always Mum's seat; she would settle in it cross-legged, while I lay sprawled on the sofa. I look at it now and imagine Mum there, Lady by her feet, while I open the package.

It's a small wooden box, with my name carved into it in Arabic. It takes me a moment to recognize the letters, but when I do my heart starts drumming. I trace them with my fingers. I open it, knowing what I'll find, because I can smell it already.

It's a perfume bottle, identical to the one Mum had. Purple, glass cut like a diamond, with a heart-shaped stopper. I untwist it and apply a drop of perfume to my skin.

I close my eyes and I get a glimpse of something. Mum's bedroom door. I know she's still there waiting for me. And I realize, in that moment, that it's not over yet. I still have a chance to finish the game, to save Mum.

Chapter 36

When I go into the game things are different. I'm outside, right across the street by the limits of the game, while a sandstorm rages around me. The wind whips me to and fro, pulling at my clothes, tearing at my hair. It wants to spin me around, to take me for a dance like it's doing with the leaves on the trees. It's so fierce it feels like it might shatter my bones. It clings to my clothes, gets into my mouth and nose. I can taste it, feel it crunch between my teeth.

I take one step, then two, but it's pulling me back away from the house.

I break my steps down.

One. Two. Three.

Just like that first day in hospital when I crossed the hall to get to Mum. I think about that and how far I've come. She's so close now. I might even be talking to her in a few minutes. And then, when I leave the game, she'll wake up.

I know she will. I can feel it.

Four. Five. Six.

We'll get to the next stage of the competition and I can tell Mum all about the game and how I saved her. She'll see that gaming is important, that it's not just a waste of time.

We'll celebrate Mother's Day at her flat, and then her birthday.

I'll ask her all about her life in Kuwait and what it was like moving to England when she was so young.

Seven. Eight. Nine.

I'm through the gate now. I'm getting closer. The silver branches surround the house entirely, sneaking through the cracks in the walls. They watch me as I walk, wriggling their bodies and hissing my name like a thousand snakes.

'*Safiya*,' they say, as if they were right next to me. '*Turn back. You're not ready.*'

'No!' I yell, gritting my teeth.

I pick up my pace, jogging now. And I finally make it through the front door.

The house is in ruins. There are no longer cracks in the walls, because there aren't any walls to begin with. The plants are all dead, the chandeliers are just shards of glass, and the bathroom is an empty pit. I glance in it, see the sink has fallen through the floor, and realize that the memory where Zaina spies on Aminah and Rawan is lost to me forever. The heartbeat of the house has slowed to a dull thud.

I rush upstairs, afraid of what I might find. What if the room is no longer there? What if Mum is gone?

But it's still there, and so is Mum.

Looking up I can see gaps in the ceiling where the roof has caved in. The stars shine down at me, winking, and the moon waves. It's like they're here to help me.

The sandstorm has disappeared now, replaced by a gentle breeze sailing through the cracks in the walls. It howls like a sad puppy waiting for its owner to return.

I stand in front of the door, memory box in hand, and wait, half expecting the door to fly open.

I wait.

And wait.

Nothing happens.

I try twisting the doorknob but it's still locked.

This can't be right. There are no more memories, I'm sure of it.

I try to say something instead. 'Mum? I have the memory box . . . I finished the challenges . . . I –' I falter. I feel silly.

Something on the other side of the house thuds against the floor, hard.

I turn, afraid. That's when the ceiling above me starts to tumble, concrete showering me in dust. I scream, and

228

glance between the door and the crumbling house. And I make my choice: I run.

I dash down the stairs, memory box in hand. Is it too late? Was I too late?

I try not to think of it as the banister crumbles to ash beneath my fingers. It's dying, the house is dying, just like Mum.

Tears stream down my face as I run out of the door, pull the gate open and dash across the street. When I finally reach the limits of the game I turn to see the world, Mum's world, crumble behind me like a sandcastle destroyed by the waves of an angry ocean.

But in one blink I'm back in the hospital, Mum sleeping peacefully next to me. The gates are replaced with curtains, the dying house with Mum's monitor, its steady beep and rhythm the only indication that she's still alive.

Nothing has changed. I didn't save her. I was wrong.

And the realization slaps me hard in the face, so hard I wish I had tumbled down, down, down with the house. I wish I had been washed away to sea like a sandcastle, or swept away by the wind.

Chapter 37

'How did it go, Saff?' Dad asks when I get into the car. He knows I was taking the memory box in today to show Mum. He doesn't know the real reason why.

'That's OK, if you couldn't show her the box today. There's more time until . . .' He can't finish the sentence, so I finish it for him. In my mind, at least.

Until we switch off Mum's ventilator.

'We can try again,' Dad says determinedly instead.

I bristle at his words. We *don't* have any more time. But he doesn't know that, because he doesn't know about the game.

When we get home Dad asks if I want to walk Lady with him. I say yes because, if I go up to my room, I'm not sure I'd ever want to leave it again.

It's dark out now and, as we walk, I relish the feeling of the frosty night air. I breathe it in, like I'm drinking a cloud. It's so different to the hot sticky air in Kuwait, which is like eating honey. Lately it's felt more suffocating than sweet, like it might swallow me whole and spit out my bones.

We walk round the neighbourhood without speaking, Dad humming a tune quietly. Lady's occasional sniffs and snorts break the silence, but it's comforting. As I tread the familiar route with them both my attention shifts to the sky.

It's something I've done since I was a child. Some people make shapes with clouds, Mum and I used to do it with stars. But I never knew, until the last memory, that this game came from my grandmother.

'What can you see?' Mum asked, our heads touching as we lay side by side on her balcony. She had a blow-up mattress and on warm summer nights she would get it out and we would lay there with a blanket, some popcorn and milkshakes.

'It kind of looks like a turtle.'

Mum lay silent while she considered this.

'Come on?' I said. 'So? What does it mean?'

'Well, this is an interesting one . . .' She paused for effect. 'Did you know some breeds of turtle travel for over 10,000 miles a year?'

'Nerd,' I said, grinning.

'How very rude!' Mum retorted. 'But also true. Anyway, do you want to know the rest, or do you want to interrupt me again?'

'Sorry, go on.'

'So, as I was saying, they travel very far each year, and that means you'll make waves in whatever you want to do. You won't give up, you'll push. And you'll win in the end.'

'I like that,' I said, satisfied.

'But –' Mum held a finger up to show she had more to say – 'you will always carry your loved ones with you, because the turtle's shell represents comfort and home. Do you think you can carry me around everywhere on your back? Shall we try it?'

I snorted. 'You made that last bit up.'

'Maybe,' she admitted. 'But I don't want you to grow up and leave me.' I could hear the pout in her voice.

'I won't,' I said. She must have been thinking about how she had left her own mum.

'Even when you're thirty?'

'Even when I'm thirty. We'll meet up for brunch or whatever it is grown-ups do.'

Mum laughed. 'And we'll talk about our annoying colleagues.'

'What else do grown-ups do?'

Mum sighed. 'Boring things like taxes and food shopping. I miss being your age. Life felt . . . endless back then, so full of hope.'

'Depressing much.'

'True, true. More popcorn?' she asked. 'And a film? You can choose this time.'

'Yeah!' I said, and I could have sworn that I saw the turtle swim across the galaxy, its body made up of stars.

I look up at the stars now. I can't see many, but a few stand out. The longer I stare and the further I walk, the smaller I feel. They're spectacular.

Mum once told me that when we look at stars we are actually looking at the past. Maybe there's a star out there somewhere from the exact year that Mum was my age. Maybe it's seen her grow up, and it'll watch me too, like our fairy godmother.

I want to hold the stars, to see them up close. I want to reach out my hand and grab them. Keep them in my pocket with the perfume, wear them round my wrist like the bracelet. Maybe then I'll be closer to her.

I think back to the memory with Aminah and her mum, and try to find the exact stars they were charting. Then I see it. The tiger, and, right next to it, the heart.

They weren't seeing different things at all, but looking at a different cluster of stars right next to one another. Tigerheart.

'What constellation is that?' I ask Dad, breaking the silence.

He squints to where I'm pointing. 'I'm not sure,' Dad admits. 'Your mum is always better at this sort of thing than I am.'

He says it naturally, but I can sense him glancing at me, second-guessing his words.

'Yeah,' I eventually say. 'She is, isn't she?'

233

And, just like that, I know what I need to do to unlock the door.

The silver branches were right: I wasn't ready. But I am now.

It's not too late.

Chapter 38

Memories are strange.

Some blur into nothing but a haze of colour.

Some blend into others until all you can remember is the memory of a memory of a memory, and you don't quite know where your imagination takes over.

And then there are other memories that are stark. It doesn't matter how long ago they happened; you remember them as clearly as if you were reliving them each time.

That's how I remember the day Mum was taken into hospital. But that's a bad memory. Good memories have that effect too.

Charlotte: GIRLS!!!

Gini: . . .

Charlotte: We did it! Our entry made it to the final!

Izzy: :0

Gini: OMG! RING ME NOW.

It's Saturday morning and Dad and I are about to go to the hospital to say goodbye to Mum.

Losing someone you love is weird. You think you'll feel sad all the time, but sometimes that's not how it is. You can find moments of happiness in between, like rays of light shining through on a cloudy day.

Saff: TEAM TIGERHEART TO WIN <3

Charlotte's news gives me strength on a day that feels like my world is ending.

The next step is for us to make a demo of the game. Then we go to London in August and present it to the *Fairy Hunters* team. And I'll be leading the presentation! Before everything that happened with Mum I wouldn't have considered it, but now I feel like I can do anything. I'm not afraid any more, like that time I got back on the horse.

'Ready?' Dad asks soon after, knocking on my open door. His voice is soft.

I remember, when I was little, screaming all the way to the hospital to get my jabs. I was terrified of the chemical smells, white walls and uniforms. Then, when we had to get our vaccinations at school, Mum would usually come to hold my hand for five minutes before returning to work.

I feel like that now. I want to scream and cry and have someone hold my hand. Dad hovers just beyond the threshold of my room, but something on my face must make him cross that line. He comes in and wraps me in his arms.

I breathe in and out, and I feel OK. Just for a moment.

'I need a few more minutes, if that's all right?'

Dad nods, retreating back out of my room, to be replaced by Lady. She doesn't do anything, just settles her head on my lap while I sit cross-legged on my floor and add the final object to the memory box.

It's a certificate with a star named after Mum. When I got home the other night I researched the constellation and found which one it was.

Luckily I had the money saved up from when I planned to book tickets to the gaming convention.

So, from now on, whenever I look at the tiger and the heart, I know that the point of the heart is called Aminah. It's sharp and full of passion, just like her.

Dad lets me go up alone when we get to the hospital. He says he'll be in the cafe.

I get to the desk and there's the nice nurse from the other night. I'm glad it's not Sue. 'She's ready for you.' She tries for a smile, but I can see her eyes are watery.

'It's OK,' I say, smiling back. And even though it isn't,

I know it will be one day.

When I walk into the room I do the same thing I've always done. I unscrew the perfume and place three drops on Mum. I watch them sink, sink, sink and, with the box in my arms, so do I.

The house is more broken-down than ever, the stairs barely standing. But I just about manage to make it to Mum's room.

The door is there, standing tall. And then I say the words I know will open it.

'I'm ready.' My voice shakes as I speak. 'I'm ready to say goodbye.'

Chapter 39

The door swings open, and a strong wind swoops past, as if the house is letting out its last breath. It's almost like it's sighing in relief, like it's been waiting for this moment for days, even weeks. And all at once the house is restored. That's how I know I'm in a memory again.

Mum's bedroom is so different to mine. Mine's much tidier, and I don't have many things. In Mum's room piles and piles of objects line the walls. Books, jewellery, boxes; photos and posters fill every gap.

The moon shines through the window, and the light falls on Mum's face, illuminating her. Her hair fans out around her, just like it does where she lies on the hospital bed. Her hands are clasped in front of her, and her face looks peaceful. I rush over to her, just as I have done countless times over the weeks.

'Mum?' I call tentatively, brushing the hair from her face.

She doesn't respond. I think back to all the fairy tales I've ever read and watched. I lean down and kiss her forehead, but she still doesn't wake.

I try something a little different. I take the perfume from my pocket. My perfume this time. I place a drop on Mum's forehead, two by each ear, and one on her neck.

The droplets sink into her skin, and the smell floats upwards, engulfing me. Wood. Rose. Orange.

All my memories with Mum and all her memories float above me like birds swooping around the room. They're as powerful as the sandstorm I walked through before. I close my eyes and remember it all.

When I next open them Mum is looking up at me, smiling. And seeing her look at me with all the love in the world makes me crumble.

'Safiya, *habibti*,' she says, pulling me in for a hug. 'Safiya, what's wrong?'

I let myself fall on top of Mum like I'm little again and we're tucked up in bed watching cartoons on a Sunday morning. I pull back, our hair intertwined so tightly it's not clear whose is whose, our tears blending together.

I rest my head on Mum's chest, and I tell her all about the game and the memories. Mum fills in the gaps with new information, and I piece her life together like all the different squares of a patchwork quilt. The stars wake up and watch over us as we talk.

'I see a tiger,' I tell her. '*And* a heart.'

She looks at me surprised, and I show her the certificate, and the rest of the objects in the memory box.

'What does it mean, Mum?' I ask when we're finished. 'To have a tigerheart?'

'It means you're passionate,' Mum explains. 'Sometimes it can go too far, and you can lose your way. But you will always find it again, because you are brave and strong and you'll never give up. Even when things are difficult.'

That's when I tell her about the competition. Mum's face lights up as she listens. 'That's wonderful, Safiya, so wonderful.' She pauses. 'I'm so sorry I didn't listen before. I was wrong to judge your interests . . . It's what my mother did before she understood, and I made the same mistake.'

I shake my head. 'No, I'm sorry,' I say, sitting up and holding her hands in mine. 'I shouldn't have said what I did about Dad and not wanting to see you. It's not true, I promise.' Then I say the words I've been waiting to say for weeks. 'I love you.'

Mum laughs, and she pulls me in for another hug. 'I know, silly. No matter how much we argue I always know that you love me.'

Dad was right.

And in that moment it feels like something lifts from my chest, like a weight had been holding my heart down in the weeks since our argument.

'I want you to come with me,' I say truthfully, while

Mum plays with my hair.

'I will,' Mum says. 'From now on I'll always be there, just like my mum was with me.'

I frown. 'When did she pass away?' I ask. I know Mum's mother isn't alive, but I never knew when she died.

'When I was your age.' Mum's voice falters then. 'She passed away soon after the play. She was sick, but she didn't tell us for a while. Her final words to me were: "Aminah, you get on that plane and you grab the world with both hands".' Mum sighs. 'I'm not sure I quite succeeded, but I tried my best.'

'You did,' I insist passionately, sitting up and facing her now. 'You're the best mum ever!'

Mum smiles, but it's sad. 'While my mum was sick, before I left for England, I used to sleep with her at night, in case there was anything she needed. She used to put a drop of perfume on her pillow before bed. That's when I had the strangest dreams of Mama at my age, except it was like I was watching a play.' Mum shakes her head, as if trying to unmuddle her thoughts. 'I thought they were just dreams but now . . .'

'You know it was magic?' I finish in a whisper, wondering whether these memories are a gift or a curse. Mum lost her mum and so have I. If that never happened, would the magic have existed at all?

We sit together for a while, and think about all that has happened, and try not to think about what is to come.

'Shall we watch some of the play?' Mum asks eventually. 'We've missed most of it now, but the next scene is my favourite.'

Mum walks me over to the window and points at her secret hideaway.

It's full of people sitting cross-legged on a great big rug. Aminah stands in front of them in her mermaid dress, Rawan by her side.

Mama and Zaina watch the play together. I see it now: the way Mama leans on Zaina for support, like she can't hold herself up.

'I remember it all so clearly,' Mum says, and then she mouths the final lines as Aminah and Rawan speak them.

When the scene is done I ask Mum how much longer we have left.

'Not long,' she admits. 'Only until the play ends.' She ushers me over to the bed. 'Let's lay together, and you can tell me all about school.'

I lie next to Mum and nuzzle up against her as we talk, eyes closed, like best friends at a sleepover. I tell her about Elle, and the book of fairy tales, and I try not to let the worry of time stop me from savouring the moment. Even though it feels like it's slipping through my fingers like sand. Because these are the final moments we have together.

'It's time, now, Safiya,' Mum says after we've chatted for a while. 'Keep your eyes closed and count to ten.'

One. Two. Three. Mum kisses me on the forehead,

brushing my hair aside.

Four. Five. Six. She squeezes my hand tight, before stepping off the bed. I do as she says and keep my eyes shut.

Seven. Eight. Nine. 'Goodbye, *habibti*. I love you.'

Ten. I open my eyes. I'm in Mum's room alone.

I run to the window and see Aminah and Rawan in their hideaway. Everyone else has gone. I can't hear what they're saying, but their laughter floats upwards through the open window, surrounding me like a hug.

I watch Aminah and how happy she is in this moment, wild curly hair blowing in the wind, eyes alight. 'I love you,' I say. 'I'll love you forever.'

The house crumbles for good, and I let it take me down with it. But I know I'll rise again, like a phoenix rises from its ashes. Just maybe not today.

I'm back at Mum's hospital bedside now, and I know it's time. I don't need to make a grand speech, don't need to say anything. I stroke the hair on her face, the bracelet dangling from my wrist, and breathe in the scent of het perfume.

I look at my mother for the last time. We'll never have the chance to make new memories together, or make up for the bad ones. But we have our old memories – good and bad – and I know they'll be imprinted in my heart for the rest of my life.

I kiss Mum on the forehead, my tears seeping into her skin.

Winning the game was never going to save Mum. I realize that now. But maybe – just maybe – it saved me.

Some days later

Lady doesn't bark when the bell rings, like she knows what's coming.

When I open the door I see them standing there: Rawan and Aunt Zaina.

'Hi, Safiya,' Rawan says, smiling, though there are tears in her eyes. Her accent is just as pronounced as I remember, and it sounds like coming home.

Aunt Zaina pulls me in for a hug. 'We're very excited to meet you,' she says, sounding exactly as she did on the phone.

Rawan has short hair, styled curly. Aunt Zaina wears a headscarf.

I smile up at my aunt and Mum's best friend. 'Hello,' I say, with confidence. 'I'm so happy to finally meet you both.'

Acknowledgements

Thank you to The Society of Authors for supporting this book with their Authors' Foundation grant.

Thank you to all of the people who helped answer my research questions; Hammad Al Najjar, for teaching me about theatre culture in Kuwait and Mark Clayton, Matthew Nichols, and Dr Andrew D Sampson for your professional medical insight. Any inaccuracies in the book are entirely my own.

A huge thank you to Claire, super-agent extraordinaire (that rhymes, which makes it official). I'm fairly certain you own a time turner because there's no other way you can possibly do everything you do. You are lovely and wise, and I want to be like you when I grow up (if that ever happens). Thank you to the rest of the RCW team: Sam for your foreign rights prowess, and Miriam for being so lovely about my silly emails.

Ali and Liz, you are a dream team. You both trusted in me at a time when I needed it most, and it is getting past that wobble (remember?) that made this book something to be proud of. Ali, thank you for your kindness and guidance; Liz, thank you for working so tirelessly on STARS and moulding my thoughts into something that made sense. Sarah L, thank you for coming in when we all needed you the most. This book would not be the same without you. Soraya, Jennie, Amy, Melissa, Lucy and everyone else in Editorial, I am so grateful for you.

Thank you to the marketing team: Jas, Sarah G, Siobhan, Hilary, Rebecca, Olivia and everyone else – you're such wonderful champions. Heather and Lizzie, thank you for designing the proof, it is so magical. Ray, Janene and Laura, I can't thank you enough for the perfect cover. I squealed when I saw it.

Before signing with an agent and getting a book deal, there was Yasmin. Everyone needs a Yasmin in their lives (preferably not mine, though). We met when our stories were picked for *A Change is Gonna Come* and have been lucky enough to see the rest of this crazy journey through together. Thank you for being my unofficial mentor and for holding my hand through this process. You are my hero. And then came Lucy. You complete our coven and I am forever in awe of your drive and talent. Thank you for inspiring Izzy's guinea pig obsession.

I have such wonderful friends, including Holly (my publishing and agency sister), Katya, Joseph, Sarah, Sam C, and the rest of the debut group – you know who you are. Then there's Rachel and Annabel, my first readers, Mariam, my first champion, and Rebecca, my first mentee. Thank you, Steph, for always being there for the cat photos and making me feel like a real-life author. Iram, thank you for listening so patiently to the plot for the failed book-we-shall-not-speak-of, and for being the best cheerleader a friend could have. Becca and Ravina, thank you for your unwavering support over the years in every way – you are both marvellous and I love that we get to watch each other stumble through life. And Danah, thank you for feeding me books in Kuwait when we were thirteen and it was difficult to find them.

Thank you to the Rentons and Co. for dealing with an unkempt, moody writer when none of this made any sense. A special thanks to Lynda and Robert for taking in a stray, and Lucy R for inspiring the crazy cat lady, designing my author signature, and keeping me (in)sane.

Dad and Diane, you believed in my dreams so completely that you were genuinely worried I was going to become too successful (before I even finished a book) and get bored of writing. Thank you for making me feel like I could do anything I set my mind to, I am utterly obnoxious because of you. Mum, thank you for my tiger heart, you'll be in my memories forever. Dana, my sweet sister, thank you for our Kuwait adventures.

Alfie, how can I possibly thank you enough? There are not enough words in the English and Arabic language combined (which I think amounts to several million) to express my gratitude for what you have done for me. You have spent many patient hours drying my tears; cradling me when I've felt lost and, when I was finally ready, helping me to fix this book over and over and over again. You have lived this all with me; the sleepless nights, the deadline stress, the meltdowns. But the good things too – the exciting emails and meetings and seeing the cover and proof for the first time. And you do it all so selflessly, without question. You are the best person I know and I love you dearly.

AISHA BUSHBY was born in the Middle East and has lived in Kuwait, England and Canada. She was the breakout star of the Stripes anthology *A Change Is Gonna Come*, alongside writers such as Patrice Lawrence, Tanya Byrne and Nikesh Shukla. She now lives by the sea and writes children's books, sometimes with a little bit of magic in them. She loves cats, gloomy days, and animated films. You can most likely find her on Twitter @aishabushby, where she spends most of her time avoiding deadlines.